As the survivor of a less than orthodox Christian upbringing, Frank Lynn is now a fully paid-up ambivalent. He can at last enjoy the charm and beauty to be found in doubt. He loves uncertainty. He is thoroughly, definitionally C of E.

Frank Lynn

THE BURNT FOOL

Copyright © Frank Lynn

The right of Frank Lynn to be identified as author of this work has been asserted by him in accordance with section 77 and 78 of the Copyright, Designs and Patents Act 1988.

All rights reserved. No part of this publication may be reproduced, stored in a retrieval system, or transmitted in any form or by any means, electronic, mechanical, photocopying, recording, or otherwise, without the prior permission of the publishers.

Any person who commits any unauthorized act in relation to this publication may be liable to criminal prosecution and civil claims for damages.

A CIP catalogue record for this title is available from the British Library.

ISBN 978 184963 544 8

www.austinmacauley.com

First Published (2014)
Austin Macauley Publishers Ltd.
25 Canada Square
Canary Wharf
London
E14 5LB

Printed and bound in Great Britain

The dog returns to his vomit and the sow returns to her mire,

And the burnt Fool's bandaged finger goes wabbling back to the fire.

Rudyard Kipling
The Gods of the Copybook Headings

For Lew, who had to start out early.

Dancing Angels, they call them, the playful little Will-o-the-wisps that finger the over-pressure. We're taught to watch for them, now, to fear them for what they portend: if you're seeing Angels, they say, you've got maybe three, four seconds to get out. They roll and pop and fizz in the churning smoke layer, pockets of gas playing peep-o as the mix reaches the sorts of temperatures at which it can auto-ignite. At about 7, 8, 900 degrees, everything's pyrolysing, sweating restless energy in to the place, working itself up to a point where the whole place might just flash over. I think of Blaenau: two of the lads basted in their own fat one workaday weekend turnout. The report said that one of them was found to have crawled in disoriented desperation back in to the heart of the fire, before his set just fell apart in the heat. It's a rage that these Angels, playing in the smog, don't seem inclined to or capable of: three, four seconds to 'I am become death, the destroyer of worlds' and they're still dancing in and out of life, gasping little asthmatics in an anaerobic primaevality, like lightning opening up moments of creation. God killing time with a lighter. Guttering little yellow breaths, stumbling forward, bowing and curtseying, and then a mesmeric, follow-me feint in to the smoke, a beautiful, beckoning Thanatos-shaped finger.

1

Must have been something like three this morning when the rain woke me, I suppose, banging on the window, insistent as a pissed up teenager. And I just lay there, for a good four or five minutes, just leaned back in to the noise and listened to it pounding away. Which is unusual for me; normally I'd have been straight up and out and stood at the window, bollock naked, eager to tap in to some of the squally violence. But not today. Little drops of water flinging themselves against the glass like Gadarene swine, and yet this morning it didn't so much as touch me. If anything, it was strangely quieting; a furious percussive drumming that, having brought me round, then flipped itself into a lulling soporific hum, its erratic waves on the panes just making the warmth and softness of the bed almost irresistible. Maybe it had something of the sublime about it – all that being beyond the reach of destructive power and stuff. Whatever. I wanted it to go on and on, sort of a heavy, cosy duvet.

It didn't disturb her, anyway. Very little does, it seems, once she's gone off. It's like having Sleeping Beauty for a bedfellow. So it wouldn't have mattered to her either way, my getting up or not, wouldn't have broken her slumber. She had her back turned to me, a full hour of glass that had worked its way out from under the quilt, and in my unheated bedroom her skin was beginning to goose pimple. She felt like I imagine sack cloth might feel, rough and coarse and slightly abrasive. Of course, she hadn't thought to bring night clothes – why would she have? There was just a navy flash of post-coitally put-back-on bra, its tired nylon being pulled into taut creases as it made the pass under her arms, where the blue stretched itself into white. I hadn't realised how broad she was, how fleshy; considerably fleshier than a back-street club's psychedelic light show had let on only a few hours ago. With pendulous breasts that evidently require night-time succour. Ignoring the fact that it felt somehow furtive, I gently fingered the tight seams of the straps, and ran a scratchy nail along them as they cut down into her cutaneous. The skin either side had ridden up like the little pink walls of a canyon, and the ridge was warm and hard under the caress of my finger. By morning she was going to be properly zippered, deep red lines of patterning circumscribing her trunk. I stroked her, tapping in to the pleasure that she was unconsciously storing up for herself, the pleasure she'd get when she finally made it home and got to go compulsive on it. But for now her ribs just continued with their rising and falling, oblivious both to my fingering and to the coming satisfaction. The mattress springs sighed in time with her breathing. And there was a little whistle, barely audible above the noise from outside, the faintest of nasal whines that accompanied each exhalation, its pitch dropping away as her lungs emptied. It's the type of tick that I know could become more than irritating if we were to try to keep this together. If, maybe, we are going to be trying. But in the moment, its whining regularity was quite endearing, a steady rhythmic counterpoint to the ebb and flow of the rain. I quite liked the idea of having somebody's irritations kicking around the place.

 It probably isn't unseasonal, in November, rain like that. And anyway, I've always liked the rub of the seasons – all the more so since I started walking it into work. I've been made to discover that it's half the enjoyment, ditching the insularity of the car to be touched by the elements. That, and being excused the enforced inertia of the Bristol Road, of course. I soon found that once you're out in a hard rain, the discomfort of the leaking and the seepage soon passes, and there's something thrilling kicks in, something atavistic, a primitive grit. Nothing speaks to the anima like arriving out of the teeth of a shit-storm. So I knew it wasn't the weather, really, even as I was lying there. Under no delusion whatsoever that the pull of the bed was down to the imperious drumming outside, that it was the unusual presence of a piece of taut nylon that had kept me away from a window. What had me spooked was what would be lying at the end of that very wet walk in.

By half-seven we were on breakfast, bacon and egg on yesterday's crusty that she knocked up whilst I showered; by the time I'd gotten to stuffing uniform into a bag, the smell of hot-grilled bacon fat had made it to the top of the stairs and was dragging me about like a nose ring. Finally I get down there and she hands it to me, and I find that she's a fellow butterer, that she puts a thick smear of the stuff all over both slices of the bread, and it mixes and runs with the warm juices of the pork and threatens to escape over your teeth and lips. Eggs just the right side of snotted. A fest of dribbling unctuousness. As I struggled with its excrescences, she went on with her wiping and tidying, moving confidently around the small space of my kitchen. I eased myself back on to the door frame and watched her, looked again upon her mass, what I'd found last night to be her comfortable substantiality. The broad run of her latissimus dorsi. And yet there she was, prancing nimbly in and out of the cupboards, deftly negotiating the poor design of their doors, the conflicted openings. So light, surprisingly light on her feet. At last she slows up a little and leans herself forward in to the sink, and her thighs press against the cold melamine and they flatten and widen and pinch themselves closed, tight, down to the knee. Made me feel a bit spoiled, somehow, to have been allowed between them, so easily, so soon.

There was definitely something of the school cook about her, what with that bustling, assured efficiency. Although she'd never before set foot in the house, obviously she'd felt sufficiently at ease to have come down and knocked this up, and then just got on with making good on the kitchen. Not even a cursory ask as to whether I actually took breakfast. Her mien slightly too settled, maybe, as she'd handed me the plate. I didn't remember any of that from last night, any sense of an inner authority, a presence. Were it not for my pressing, 0-nine-hundred-hours engagement with a fire engine, I wondered whether the morning might not have begun stretching itself out into that space where it gets awkward and slightly threatening.

But of course I did have to be going. As I guided her out into the porch and closed the door to, she slipped her hands into my back pockets and squeezed the cheeks of my arse, her head cocked and flirty. It was the cook again, or matron, I think her way of trying to take charge of the moment, the parting scene, the frame before the tumbling weed of '... so, do you fancy meeting up next week, sometime?' A passive-aggressive demand for some sort of indication of intent. At the very least it was a request that I slow up a bit, and notice the coy little smile with which she was smiting me. She tasted of brown sauce and bacon, as I leaned in to kiss her, a luscious saucy porcine salute to the last eight or ten hours of our time together. My hands were already there, gently cupping her head as an adjunct to the kiss, but with sex brought so close it was inevitable that they'd go in search of her again, in search of that fullness, of the topographical interplay between her generous body and its weary gilding. The stitching of her skin. They lingered for a while, once more back and forth, chasing down the whiteness of the seams – just refamiliarising themselves – and then we kissed again, long and slow and indifferent to clocking-on times, and her eyes sparkled. I tidied a wayward lock of hair: 'Thank you. Especially for the indulgence. Though I think it was probably a little reckless of you, on a first date.'

'Maybe it was. Maybe next time I should object.'

'Next time it won't be a first date.'

She'd finished with my arse, though not before finding my car keys for me, which she dangled in front of me like a tease.

'God, I don't even know where you live. Can I drop you off somewhere, on my way in?'

*

I park up at the Bear. Have done since Bertie foisted his inane bus lane on us, and made a pedestrian out of me. But I'm no St. Paul; my Damascene moment involved more than a little coercion, and it certainly didn't leave me blind to the convenience of the combustion engine. And what's getting irksome is that I relive it, that morning of my conversion, I relive it every time I ditch the car here to walk in.

Of course, when I first heard they were planning a bus lane along here I wasn't that bothered, even though it was likely going to mean ten, fifteen minutes onto the journey. It's the Bristol Road, for God's sake – the arthritic shuffle, the grinding attrition of red lights and green lights is what we do. Bored resignation sort of sets the tone for those of us whose preferred working-day default is numb. And I've got nothing against the buses themselves, per se, though given the choice I'd rather pogo it into town than catch one. But that's just a personal space thing; good luck to those amongst us who aren't so picky, who are willing to bunk up and who no doubt love to drag all that eager gregariousness into work with them. Buses should be allowed to expedite the righteous on their way.

A good two years ago, then, when they put it in. At least two years, and yet it's still so clear in my head that it might have been yesterday. It was one of those brilliant aurorae that January occasionally throws you to take the edge off weekdays, something like an apology, almost, for all the cold, dark starts. Everything out there just saturated in colour, irradiating colour, all of it breaking out like the first morning, with or without blackbird's say-so. As crisp as a creative day. Even the log-jam of traffic, when I rounded the bend by Manor Drive and saw it all, concertinaed rows of boots and bumpers already backed up way past Weoley Park, and all of them in front of me, between me and where I needed to be – even then, the only thing that really registered was the way they shimmied in the sun's Glorious Technispray. You could have been forgiven, briefly, for thinking it had all been planned, a sort of cosmic-council collaboration designed to mollify the Great Unmoving.

And up to that point I was pretty easy about it; even as I drifted to a slow stop and assumed the inert position, I was quite happy to be sat there. More than a little bemused as well, obviously, as to how pinching everything down to a halt like this was going to help the world's polar bores. But I reckon the only thing I had to annoy me at that stage was the faint whiff of exhaust fumes which had started to filter in, playing with my tongue and nostrils, that claggy taint that seems to affix itself to all your soft, moist respiratory bits. Pulled up too close to the Beamer in front, I just let the car roll back a foot or two, and watched rather than breathed the steady stream purring out of her twin exhausts. I remember it billowing and turning opaque the moment it hit the morning cold, and then lifting like an offering of incense. Made me smile, and think of the oblation that I, too, would have been sending up to the God of Misguidance.

Of course it was always going to be short-lived; it lasted all of five, ten minutes, my laid-back introduction to Bertie-the-Layer-of-Bus-Lanes and his attempts at traffic management. You'll know everything there is to know about bus lanes by now, surely, about how that vacancy of tarmac to the left seems to exert an almost planetary pull on shit. As I say, plays in my head as though it were yesterday. I'd already moved on from the stuff coming out of its exhausts to the Beamer's driver, and the pout of pomegranate-red with which she was filling her rear-view. The intensity with which she applied the finishing touches. A crimped pucker, and then she expanded her mouth into a voluminous black hole that she orbited with a thin tail of lipstick. They were full lips, Mae Wests, and now florid and sanguine; intentionally suggestive, I was beginning to think, excited ... and then that lowered Clio punctured it, shifting down the empty inside lane, no attempt at disguising her contempt, no attempt to look bus-like. Bouncing off her spoiler as she slipped by, our glorious January sun suddenly becoming nothing more than an insouciant solar wink, a bright solar finger. A provocation, it seems, that few of them were able to resist: as soon as she'd popped her Clio-shaped enema up there, there was shit flowing down that bus lane in waves. Everywhere, I could feel polar bears leaping everywhere.

It shouldn't have bothered me that much; I'd allocated time enough to get in to work, with or without the solipsistic world-view of the Clio brigade. I suppose I would have been a little pissed at how brazenly they asserted their time sheet primacy. But it was their animus that really got to me, and that would eventually convince me of the inevitability of the pedestrian way: that they could actually be so indignant that we queuing might dare object to being jumped when the bus lane filtered them back in, an indignation they conveyed with rabid eyes and spittled lips and a round of fucks, and which they prosecuted at the preformed-plastic point of imperious offside bumpers. Every morning, without fail, without let-up, and all of it performed to a dissonant horn chorus.

For a while you offer some sort of token resistance, by way of hugging up to the bumper in front, maybe even believing it to be a kind of public service, an act of moral propriety. A sanitary act. And just finding something over to the right on which to be focusing while you're being *fucker*-ed from the left. But unless you're a zealot, the moral aspect of fairness quickly cedes to the pragmatic when you realise that to confront them all is to turn a six-mile commute into the judgement of Sisyphus. The effluent will still come, morning after morning, no matter how much of it you shut out, no matter how much shit you roll up that hill. But of course then there is a cost of not rolling, a payment levied less at the point of contact than more generally, more subliminally. When giving way starts to become the default, inevitable reaction to a looming bumper, the feeling of being slightly diminished sticks with you for the rest of the day, and the day is somehow sullied. The quality of shitness is transferred. 'God bless those bloody bears' was pretty much the only response I could come up with, towards the endgame, along with 'God bless Bertie', who, with a quick flick of his council house biro, had managed to auteur our everyday, accepted tedium into something Ypric.

I endured must have been about six months of this, at the end of which I'd be finding myself in the station car park for ten minutes before the start of every shift, coming down, trying to recapture some of my precious, pre-bus lane numbness. And it was about then that I realised I was just too old to be playing with faeces. He'd won. Bertie had beaten the car out of me.

So, its unimpeachably green credentials notwithstanding, I started walking it. Jehovah's Witnesses walk. Even ex-

Jehovah's Witnesses. It's what they've been trained to do. Although, despite my years of training, I actually walk only part of it, which is certainly recalcitrance over Bertie, and maybe over JWs, too. I drive the first couple of miles and then leave the car at the Bear and Staff, which is pretty well where it all begins to choke up. It's an ideal dump spot; at a decent pace, the walk in only takes about forty-five minutes, and it has a car park sprawling enough for a landlord not to be so bothered about a beaten up Mazda tucked away at the far end. Ideal, once I'd managed to disconnect the place from Effie.

*

By about ten-to, I'd dropped her off and then gotten myself over to the pub. The storm was pretty much spent at that point, but shit had she enjoyed herself last night. Ok, the three-o'clock wake-up call might have prepared me for a little post-inclemency debris, as had some of the drive over, but pulled up here, now, the intensity of that fury was almost chastening. Especially when I thought back to that delicious comfort, that almost seductive duvet wooing of only a few hours ago. Seems she'd taken a particular dislike to the poplars, a dozen or so of which form themselves up into something of a perimeter on the Bristol Road side, somebody's idea of a token screen against the congestion. Tall and insubstantial at the best of times, they'd always looked to me like so many of the destitute, a quiet line outside a soup kitchen. But she'd evidently spent the night on them, slapping them about and stripping them out, an intemperate Boreas, to leave them looking ragged and forlorn, cowed even. Just in front of them – just in front of me – the fence lay sucker-punched across the driveway, so even had the car park not been turned into a make-shift mortuary for poplar limbs, I couldn't have gotten to my usual spot, over away on the left, far enough from the pub itself to make investigating it seem less than worthwhile. And everywhere the requisite plastic bags, caught up in what was left of the trees or pinned into doorways, or still tumbling around the place, a few of them, like crap-table dice.

I suppose the drive over was still on – it just would have meant me having to get off my arse to shift the fence and then some of the bigger stuff, the woody consequence, picking a ginger way through all the post-apocalyptic squall. But it struck me as being even less discreet than just dumping the car up by the entrance and hoping that the landlord wasn't going to choose today, of all days, to have a downer on fly parking. Sixty quid for a wheel clamp, I was thinking as I locked it up, or who knows how much if it gets towed. Not that I had any choice, what with Old Joe's bell beginning to mark off the morning with the first of his eight chimes; had to be going. Had a day to face.

The doors of the bar were wide open as I came past them, and at first I made an effort to quieten the rubberized squelching of my boots on the wet paving slabs, but then it seemed pointless, a moment's silence against the great green sulk of a car that was going to be sat there for the staring at, sat there provoking him, for the next nine or ten hours. And of course it was nothing but displacement, anyway, this boots thing, another distraction presenting itself, to be gotten through, much like the morning's permutations on swine, like the thin diversion of waif-trees and wheel clamps. An occupied mind cycling through and attaching itself to fluff, trying to avoid the room's elephant. But of course I knew, as I let my boots noisily loose on the Bristol Road, I knew as I'd known from long before any three o'clock arousal that this might turn out to be the walk that sees the unravelling of my ambulatory conversion. Every moistly resonant step along here was another step into the unknown.

Kwesi Simpson. That's the name unknown goes by; though he's unknown to us only insomuch as we hadn't actually had him as our gaffer before. And, of course, it's not really an unknown unknown. Stuff percolates through, inevitably, stuff gets whispered: his predilection for grandstanding oratory at big exercises; the five kids that he has tagging along to every function, testament, maybe, to his reproductive prowess; the cock extension that is his Honda NSX.

He was to be starting in less than an hour, and by all accounts, he doesn't start well. When he was put in charge of Sheldon Green Watch, a couple of years ago, there was no introductory first-morning chit-chat, no 'Hi, I'm Kwesi, this is how it's gonna be, make it so'. Just a sullen imperative to get out into the yard, where they spent the next two and a half hours performing variations on the same tired old fire brigade routines: a thirteen-five ladder to the third floor, a main jet working into the tower. As though he were asserting himself, one of the blokes said, an imperious concern with projecting his power. Strange – if it's true – for such a big, physically imposing bloke. Ironic. Something slightly unbalanced about him, they'd said. But it seems insecurity sets out a pretty tedious stall; every shift, apparently, they'd be out there jumping through the hoops of his flawed psychology, come rain or shine, running through the same basic combinations. In less than an hour. I couldn't wait. The joy of perfunctory drill, repeated ad nauseam because the guy would seem to possess neither the creative nous nor the self-confidence to run a watch.

I met him once. Or rather, I found myself in the same room as him, eavesdropping as he expounded to some guy that he'd cornered his views on mess tables. Evidently the seating arrangements at dinner are something of a pet fetish of his. Every station I've ever been on, the mess tables are pushed together into a square or rectangular unit around which all of the boys sit, together, just getting on with it. Isn't that the idea, the whole point of it? We all get thrown in there, and bump and grind along, a disparate amalgam out of which something eventually coalesces and emerges, something like a functioning watch. But it would appear he has this thing about the cliquiness of watches, about how they need to be made to be more inclusive, more friendly, and so he likes to break it all up and fracture the seating into paired tables. Dot them around the room, he was saying, separate them out so it's no longer suggestive of a working environment, but is more like a restaurant that you might choose to walk into and eat at. Reconfigure the setting, and just sit back and watch as the behaviour changes accordingly. He was nodding earnestly, the poor bloke on the receiving end of this, while doubtless trying to disguise his bemusement. For God's sake, Pavlov, I was thinking, it's a fire station; we've no choice but to be there for the duration of the shift. And while I'd be the first to admit that not every watch is quick on extending the welcoming handshake, I just couldn't see the logic behind any of it, this little plan of his. How does it work? How is shackling a couple of blokes to each other at a table supposed to synthesize some sort of chumminess out of indifference?

That he's a romantic, I can put up with. I've had worse. But then there's all that stuff about nitty-gritty, which, after someone pointed out is another of his hobby-horses, I'm suddenly discovering I use all the time. Hadn't even realised it, that I had become so reliant upon a succession of hackneyed verbal tics to get me through a sentence, hadn't realised that my arguments were quite so flabby and unmarshalled. Apparently he lives to take people to task over their use of it, however innocuously they use it, however correct their grammar, because it is definitely a description of the slave detritus in the hulls of transatlantic slavers, and any flippant or non-contextual use is an offensive trivialisation of the entire slave experience. Even though it definitely isn't. So what's next, Little Miss Obloquy? 'Niggardly'? 'Empirical'? We're all of us in here slaves, I found myself muttering at a post-squally Bristol Road, every man jack one of us.

The wind was back, starting to snatch at my hood, and had me wondering whether in fact she had life in her yet. A couple of the drains down here had already been overwhelmed, and great pools of water were straddling the road and pavement, rubbing out the curbs and gutters for stretches, hundreds of yards at a time. The cars are always backed up anyway, when you get this close to town, but in the absence of anything by which to orient themselves they were slowed to a crawl, their drivers ploughing hopeful lines through the flood water. The displacement of the tyres sends out rippling little spasms, little crests that rush and race themselves to the edges of the water, where they then just peter out and die. And in between, when a red traffic light gives it all a break from the churning of the wheels, it manages to catch the reflection of the street lamps and headlights and tail lights on its viscous, racing skin, swatches of bobbing colour coming down after something like epilepsy. Blinking convulsions of colour. The reflection of a louring sky adds a dramatic intensity to it all, a spectacular pulsing intensity; an hypnotic little lightshow played out in a grubby body of water sat on top of a storm drain.

As I picked my way along the tidemark, I was determined not to let him ruin all of this, to deprive me of these little moments that flash out from the everyday. If push comes to shove, I don't doubt I can still do it, all of the mental attrition bullshit. I've done time enough to appreciate that they can't but come with a need to make their mark. The arrival of any new gaffer is an organic process, an evolution of adaptation and compromise in which they seek to impose and you try to yield in the direction in which you want them to push. All the little quirks and oddities that they tend to accumulate are just the collateral damage, I suppose, of them trying to keep the peripatetic posts of Fire Brigade promotion in focus. But it still left me out of sorts as I negotiated the debris of a late autumn area of low pressure. I don't do out of comfort zone stuff, any of this breezy striding into an adventurous off-piste. His keenness, his toeing the company line, our having to negotiate his willy-waggling – all of it was intruding upon my walk, the way I knew it was going to. 'Bunny' they called him over there, at Sheldon, the 'Jungle-' obviously unvoiced. From what I hear, 'Hyperactive Twat' would have been easier, or 'Dickhead Drill Pig' – less of a peering into unemployment. Why flirt with it? But of course the subversive power of a piss-take is pretty much proportional to how close it sails to a taboo, to how closely the words that you speak come to the unspeakable. And if they'd been rumbled, they'd always have had the easy get-out of the coney connexion, the at-it-like-a-rabbit fertility that he seems concerned with parading, and which they would no doubt have delivered with an aggrieved relish, eyebrows innocently raised and wronged arms outstretched. Or sometimes they'd just play the Simpson card, and call him 'OJ'. Kwesi Simpson – I practised it, formed it up, tried to think of it without any baggage because pretty soon I was going to have to voice it without any baggage. Kwesi Simpson, for what was left of the journey in to work. Bunny. I'm generally wary of buying wholesale into reputations, or at least I like to think I make the attempt: he'll no doubt stand or fall on his Jack Jones in the first week or so. But what with so much smoke and fire... Kwesi Simpson. It's got a pleasing rhythm to it, an echo of balancing assonance in the chiasmus in which Old and New Worlds are fused. I imagine it as an incantation, an ululating background soundtrack as Bob Geldof pontificates to camera or something. Which should probably set me to wondering whether I've already started buying.

And then I have a horn sounding out from somewhere behind, an aggressive monosyllable that pierces through the damp to level out the nascent ululating. Quite when or why the moist glories of this morning had taken a wrong turn back there, to lead me into the fraught dark alley of identity politics, I couldn't be sure of, but on balance I was glad of the wake-up. The confluence of Belgrave Middleway and the Bristol Road is bleak enough without added OJ. I especially hated this bit of the drive, after Bertie had finished with it. The grimness of the city as it seeps southward has an almost ideological bent to it, I'd always thought that; a masochistic Soviet austerity. But being forced to look out over the view here, out over this suppurating concrete city-scrape for what seemed like custodial lengths of time, to then have a succession of hobos drop into the line as if just hopping off a bus-lane boxcar, only hastened the end. Hated it. And the slightest recollection of that driving-in hatred never but gives my walk a bounce now, an energetic cadence that I suspect may well come across as insufferably preachy, if you've been sat in traffic for an hour.

It still yields nothing, cedes not a thing to the lived experience of the people round here. Still the same soulless high-rise, low-socio housing, with tenants that daily have their rhythms and routines subordinated to the Middleway and its bollards and barriers and underpasses, as it works its remit to just keep the rush hour moving. A city-sized experiment in the collectivisation of the will. So it must really piss them off, even as they suffer all this inconvenience in deference to the Greater Moving Good, that for so much of the time everything's all chronically gridlocked anyway. As a means to get to B, it's a fucking sick, slow geodesic. And what really riles me is that one of Bertie's predecessors – father of Bertie – had thought to sanction a McDonald's there, right on the junction; a 'drive thru', right there where there was for so much of the time a singular lack of driving, period. A gaudy neon sign that taunted us with verbs of motion as we sat there, motionless, before and within and contributing to the dystopian landscape. Nice touch, that, I thought, and with a sense of the deliciousness of irony denied to his boy. Three-quarters of an hour of gridlock, in which my frustration would have found relief only in an occasional impotent raging, and the moment I saw it I couldn't keep that lilting descant out of my head. Oh, yeah, 'I'm lovin' it', alright.

But I suppose it's a little more lovable now. Or it is for me; I still don't see a great deal of love anywhere else, in the joyless faces of the commuting columns and rows, in the glaze of the eyes. Give or take the odd aberrant horn, everything's just resignation, all of it a powered down, survival instinct dormancy. An emotional atrophying. Perhaps being closeted in the safe, warm confines of a passenger compartment doesn't allow for a connexion, for any visceral appreciation of the elements at play: the colours of the traffic lights that jam it all up here also bob and duck and dance in the puddles, too, swatches of colour that seem just as eager to entertain as were the ones further back. Even the shittiness of the reflected skyline that flits in and out of the view manages to look a little less rigidly Russian when you have an elemental breeze whipping a few spots of Brummagem spit into your face.

But I can't bounce, I must not bounce the walk down here. I'd look like a cock, yes, but it's more than that. What's particularly unnerving about all the listlessness and stupor around me is that it must have been my stupor only a matter of months ago. I would have been sat here, with Bristol Street no more than sixty feet away, looking at it snaking off into town with barely a set of wheels on it, and separated from it by nothing more than a change of lights. Just like this lot, who are sat at the front of what is effectively a three-mile queue, having spent an age getting to this point, about to be let go on their way, released, liberated, and yet they're still just formed up in row after sedated, doleful row, pressing themselves up against the white line to stare vacantly ahead. Eyes dead, every one of them. And these would have been my eyes, too? As flat as these, as blank and as unresponsive to life around? One of the Berties has even put in an extra lane or two for the final quarter of a mile, so as to pack as many lugubrious faces in there as possible. Insensitive, I know, but as I'm looking at them I can't help but think of that picture of those Jews pressed up against the Buchenwald wire, looking blankly back at incredulous GIs.

As I get close to the crossing they move off, initially a slow shuffle in response to the green light that's just flashed up, but it builds as I stand there watching. A massed will takes a while to mobilise itself. But it's soon at full steam, a freight of rubber and steel and indifference pouring past, sucked forward by the vacuum before it, pushed forward from behind, elongating and stretching itself out, less like a train I suppose than a universe expanding itself into the space available to it. An awesome surge of Big Bang. Raging by. And then, just as it seems ineluctable and overwhelming, the cautioning amber appears, the red. That grinding attrition. And there is something Pavlovian about *this*, as they slow and stop, something conditioned and lemming-like. At last the diminutive green man pops up to invite me over, assuring me with that jaunty little goose-step of his that it's okay, now, suddenly, to just step out in front of all that insentient power. He has me feeling like Moses, suddenly able to hold back my very own Red Sea with nothing more than a little red light bulb for a shekinah light: 'and the children of Israel went into the midst of the sea upon the dry ground: and the waters were a wall unto them on their right hand', though not, for this Moses anyway, also 'on their left'. For the twenty paces of the crossing, I am the anointed of the Lord, once more.

It's an unfamiliar feeling these days, walking with the Lord, and it certainly beats all that anxiety over new gaffers. But the ludic distraction of my Moses cameo pulls me not towards memories of being saved but to the screen-wash women that I've just noticed for the first time, bobbing up and down on my Red Sea, little Egyptian charioteers and pharaohs riding the crests. They weren't there when I used to drive in; there was nothing – other than Clios in bus lanes – either to upset our torpor or offer us distraction. But they're here now, three or four of them picking their way in and out of the cars with their cheap chamois and dirty water, distilling the apathy. Or perhaps catalysing it into something. Though they seem pretty inured to it, pretty indifferent to the indifference, if that's what it is, which is I suppose the self-preservation of the indentured. And, of course, these aren't Egyptian charioteers tossed about on the Lord's oceanic vengeance but little Romanian ones, or Polish or Czech, migrant flotsam beached up on angry shores. Which extended mixed metaphor, I know, makes me an honorary Jew manufacturing concentration-camp Jews out of jammed cars, and vengeful armies out of penury. Trebly insensitive. But that's the legacy of fundamentalism for you, colours everything you see and do.

2

The voice was familiar enough, weaselling its way up the stairs to meet me. Difficult not to recognise it really: it's a pretty distinctive nasal whine he's got going on, has Nigel. Which is in itself irritating enough. But it's his habit of chewing on his hard palatals that really grabs you, as soon as you notice it, and that has you running ahead of whatever crap he's coming out with, as you try to anticipate when the next one might pop up. 'She so gives me the tchwinge, with those fuck-off big Bristols of hers. How I'd love to paint the space betchween them', where his really dropping down into the double-u accentuates the otiose 'ch'. His lips lift and come forward as he forms it, puckering up as though he's about to snog you with one of his cheap laddisms. Always struck me as being a rather pointless affectation, at once self-aggrandising and needy, although I suppose it rather complements the pointlessness that is his humour. Or perhaps it's a childhood thing, picked up off the back of some sort of trauma, a little tic that rides around on him, unbeknown to him. Overactive lip muscles. Parasitized levator labii. But whatever – there could be no mistaking it, projecting out of the locker room the way it always does when he's about. I can't stand the tchwat, I really can't, but somewhat counter-intuitively I've conditioned myself to look forward to the sound of him: the brief unpleasantness of Nigel-noise signals that my working week is about to finish. So it threw me, initially. This wasn't his day. That drip, dripping of self-congratulatory laughter shouldn't have been sounding off anywhere near here, not yet – Red Watch weren't due on again until ... Monday. And yet here he was, pressing himself much too early into my working week.

I was only out there to get a little respite from OJ. After almost an entire day of him, his co-opting our five o'clock break to foist even more fire brigade bollocks on to us had been the camel-snapping straw. Ok, maybe that's a little unfair; he'd been a bloody nause, yes, but so far only because of an evidently natural predisposition of his to hyperactivity. No nastiness; there'd been no willy – not yet, anyway. But I'd needed a bit of space. And all it had taken was the excuse of a toilet break and I was out and making a dash down to the locker room. And then I have that twat's masticating bringing me up short.

But of course I should have known, given what today is, given how important today has become to everybody. We *do* charity. So it would have been a pretty good bet, really, that his squeaking self was going to have been putting in an appearance sometime over the course of the evening. And pretty likely, too, that I'd be finding myself rubbing up against him at some point during it. When you've however reluctantly agreed to be a pooled charitable resource, you don't always get to choose who'll be rattling the bucket next down the line.

So there I was, stopped on the stairs, suddenly feeling like the Grand Ol' Duke, give or take a man. It was a zero-sum predicament: carry on down and have Nigel ruin my time out, or about face and go back up to where OJ was still holding court. And so have no time out anyway. Kwesi or the cock – like flipping a double-tailed coin.

The nose was announcing '...perfect timing' as I came through the open doorway. Made me falter, ever so slightly, but there again it was unlikely to have been directed at me: how could he have anticipated my coming in, with that sort of choreography? 'Serendipitous, even. A whole swag-bag of serendipity.' So I didn't rise to it, but let the creaking of my locker hinges interject, hoping that they might ruin whatever dramatic effect he'd been building up to. Quite why he was sat there declining nouns, I couldn't be arsed to ask. He was perched on the shabby table against which we cock a leg when our shoes need a quick, pre-parade wipe; evidently he thought it had the makings of a suitable stage. The necessary portentous drum-roll he provided courtesy of a black biro. 'Don't you think that it's *fortchewitous*?' I wondered abstractedly whether this is why I don't like him, why so many of them – even the blokes off his own watch – seem less than easy about him. He just doesn't appear to be aware of what a prick he is, how random it is for him to be declaiming into nowhere stuff that no-one seems to understand or is interested in, without context or preamble. They all just try to avoid eye contact. Self-awareness he isn't. 'That he's turned up *today*, of all days? Just in time for this evening's *stick up*?' Ah, so, eventually we get there: this is his take on Kwesi's arrival. Thank you for sharing. I couldn't begin to imagine how much of his day must have been spent coming up with it, this elliptical riff on the implied extorting efficacy of our new gaffer. Given the epic self-regard, maybe I should've just been grateful that his thesaurus routine had actually reached a dénouement at all. Serendipity? Nigel, I thought, you're less than interesting. Most of the blokes in here will have switched off at the first syllable, cryptic or otherwise, you annoying nob.

I suppose about a dozen or so had made the effort, boys off the other watches who, like him, had come in to lend a collective collecting helping hand, to rattle a tin for Terry. Tonight was Wogan's annual incarnation as wing man to Pudsey, and given the caring, sharing image our employer likes to project, we're encouraged to get caught up in the cross-fire. For at least the last ten years or so, the appearance of a disfigured soft toy has been our cue to kick off the mugging that is Children in Need. And all those poor unfortunates attempting to negotiate a way home through the snarl-up of rush hour get the added joy of us, descending on them with an intimidation of outstretched buckets and helmets, and a weight of moral expectation. Most of them, I seemed to recollect from last year, are by then looking like Commuters in Need, of their dinner, and a beer, probably, and certainly of respite from a bunch of firemen whose presence can only but remind them that it's a Friday night, already gone six, and they're still stuck in town.

And he'd be expected to take charge of it, Kwesi, as the gaffer, no matter that he'd started only a few hours earlier. He'd have had no choice over it. You rock up and take it on, whatever happens to be there in the diary. So tying up all the loose ends, the who was to be collecting where, all the safety stuff, organising coffee, the cash – it would all have been thrown in his lap the moment he'd come through the door. We were expecting ... at least a little disorientation. But he wasn't even in the slightest bit fazed by it. He hit the ground at nine o'clock and in a vortex of energy and can-do swept up everything in that swollen in-tray of his, leaving the shell-shocked rest of us spinning in his slipstream. That was the stall he set actually out; from the off, from the moment we'd sat down for a morning brew, he'd been a fatiguing, overbearing, bouncy maelstrom of zeal. I suppose we couldn't but have seemed a little muted, in the face of it. Though perhaps that was just our confusion, having found ourselves upstairs in the mess room rather than out on the yard. But God, by eleven, I was almost willing him to notice the tables, to be distracted just for a moment by all that latent cliquiness.

And he was still holding court at five-ish, and with our tea-break, which is to take the piss. Evidently he'd had time enough by then to get on top of it all, and was busily outlining everything that he thought we might achieve and ought to be aiming for. Enthusiasm, apparently, is infectious, and it electrifies a donating public. Certainly, last year's figures were good – this as he vigorously whisked a very black coffee – all the more impressive given the rain that dampened your bucket-rattling importuning, and yes, there is this time round all sorts of talk of compassion fatigue, but come on, we do some of our best stuff under pressure, we don't shy from challenge, we don't blah, blah, blah... Bless him, people pay hundreds for this type of motivational guff. The guy must live his life as a perpetual pep talk, never venturing out of that solipsistic bubble of his that admits of no failure. After eight hours in his eternal sunshine, I'd needed to find a little shade. Hence the attempt at escaping out to the locker room. I'd quietly closed the door on him faffing over whether or not it'd be better to go down in the mini-bus. It's half a mile at most. Pushing through the fag end of the rush hour, squeezed into a van with a gaffer no-one had yet decided if they liked or not, or walk it.

*

Before today, if you'd found some sort of reason to ask, I'd have said that ours was probably the least suggestible of any watch on the station, collective proof of the futility of either the subliminal or the coercive. And yet still he was hitting us as we paraded off at six, a rousing peroration that I fear we may find is something of a speciality of his. Tight, focused and to the point, I'd thought as I stood there in the face of it; practised, and used to getting results. Fortunately it was Green Watch's parade, so he hadn't time for anything extended – just finished off the working day with 'three hundred quid to get the better of. Come on, lads, we can do this, with just a little fire brigade brio. Go *infect* them.' His eyes were sparkling with it all. 'In five minutes, by the front door?' And then a couple of the boys were straight over to it and waiting for him, without even bothering to change.

Was it surprise? Or is it that I'd felt something give, something like a crumbling of certainty? At least Bob had demurred, thank God, heading off to the locker room as normal, seemingly immune to OJ's expectations but perhaps somehow attuned to the fragility of my own. I'd felt the need to give those ringing invocations a moment. As I turned to follow him through, the gaffer off Green Watch caught me by the shoulder and indulged me in a parody of a massage, his clumsy thumbs limning at something buried, beyond the knotty trapezius that he was playing with. And then an avuncular, wise old owl nod. In the sparkling he'd obviously seen confirmation of what he'd been seeking, the comfort of the cliché, the easy truth of rumour: 'Welcome to the rest of your career, Big Boy. How are you at pacing yourself?' And this was their *Gaffer*. I managed a pretty wan smile: 'It's a couple of hours shaking a tin for kids, for God's sake – maybe the guy was a bloody orphan.'

There was nothing for the locker hinges to silence this time, when I got there, nothing for them to compete with but the silence, but in that quick metallic squeal there was just enough of a touch of the familiar to steady me, a reaffirming reassertion of the status quo. Something reliable, something everyday. Bob was by then changing out of his undress uniform, with that slow little ritualistic disrobing of his: always the trousers first and then his tie and his shirt, each of them laid over the open door of his locker before he puts on his civvies, and then hangs up his uniform for the next shift. Slowly, deliberately, same way he always does, untouched by the events of the day. His just being there was a steady, taciturn bulwark against the room's emptiness, what would otherwise have been its quiet reproach. Ballast in a shit storm.

Earlier, Kwesi had paired us up to hit on the out-of-town carriageway, which was pretty much the same detail that we'd had last year. It'd all seemed so different, then, enjoyably different, despite the showers; we'd spent most of the evening working up our pincer, where Bob would distract them by trawling ostentatiously down from the lights in full view, whilst I came up on them from behind. And we'd had the craic all evening on it, bouncing off the punters right up until the last half-hour or so. And only when the boredom had started to creep in, only when it'd gotten stale and tedious, only then had he suggested a little wager, ten quid to see which of our approaches made for the more generous benefaction, altruism or ambush. It had been three hours or so of charitable cheer. And yet tonight, however fatigued their compassion might be, I couldn't help thinking that it would end up outweighing my own. It's a couple of hours; why then the creeping cynicism? Why did I suddenly feel like my life had been taken over by a petty grudgingness?

That infectious thing again. It felt almost as though he'd hand-picked it, knowingly, deliberately, picked it to be the day's constant refrain: 'And he saith unto them, saith again and again and a-bloody-gain, Come, follow me, and I will make you fishers of men'. Of men's pockets. *The contagion of belief.* Something like an incantation. Believe in the Fire Brigade, believe in the power of the good, in spending three or four hours out in the cold with a tin. Be there. Of course, for most of us the association should have tainted it from the off: Fire Brigade advocacy of anything like this is usually predicated on someone's having a career to burnish, on some needy soul's need to garner a little kudos unto themselves, a small willy needing waggle-help. But surely this reluctance of mine must be more than just an aversion to Fire Brigade solipsism. Perhaps it was the intensity of his simple truth, his certainty, his casual assumption that we surely must believe that which he believes. The expectation, never other than smiled, the gentle but inexorable radiation of a pressure that seeps out and around you and is then suddenly over you and upon you as a soft yet smothering, nurturing but strangulating umbilical. A couple of hours for kids? How can you argue against it when it's laid bare before you like that, a bald assertion of monochromatic truth? But I've been at the sharp end of necessary truths before, the a priori first principles upon which people have their lives stripped out and sequestrated. The initial capitulation, the unforeseeing acceptance of that plausible first premise, and upon this rock shall I build my church.

We couldn't have been in there more than ten minutes, Bob and I. But by the time we'd divested ourselves of those Fire Brigade vestments of ours, most of the others had piled out and were spilling down the hill in twos and threes, a Kwesi-headed sliding scale of ... I don't know, of commitment to this thing? Commitment to him? Whatever. Anyway, that to which we were or were not committing ourselves lay west, and we headed out into the last of the sun's weak warmth. It was touching up the sides of the tower blocks as it went down, Studley and Wilmcote and Brinklow, making them flush a peachy pink, as though we'd stumbled in upon something clandestine, some inappropriate fumbling, and they were unsure whether to be embarrassed by us or defiant. I didn't know whether they'd seen it, the little gaggle of the eager at the front. Judging by the pace they'd set, they couldn't have been focused on much other than getting down there, to sort out the job in hand. OJ's infectious Exocet sense of purpose.

He'd hurried them down as far as the crossing. It's nothing more than a perfunctory slash across Highgate Middleway, but a necessary slash, given the speed of the traffic that comes this way. The whole of the planning around there is kinetic – too kinetic, I came to think, after I'd attempted to cross it a few times. I'd found that that bouncy, proselytizing stride of mine had segued easily into jaywalking ennui, until one morning I'd come close to realising my statistical potential. So the hundred yards that is the detour to the crossing became an essential if annoying dogleg, all the more so for its being such an uninspired effort when you actually get to it: nothing more than half a dozen randomly planted trees of some nondescript variety, a few of them huddling together to take the edge off the horizon, off the verticality of those tower blocks beyond. And a twin-run of galvanized railings, to escort you across the reservation as though you can't be trusted not to stray. Funnelling you through the bald run of the turf, through the general aesthetic austerity of the view – the occasional coyness of tower blocks excepted. A lone berberis has made itself a bleak home there, by the side of the railings, its thin limbs reaching through the bars like a huddle of convicts reaching out of a B-movie. But counter-intuitively it makes it all less institutionalised, somehow, and not more. In the small space that it's carved out, amidst the debris of McDonald's and Silk Cut washing up on to the little earth wall of the embankment, there seems to be regeneration and reclamation, not internment. Or that's how I see it, anyway. I'm not sure that they saw it at all, either the green or the grey, or even the pink, as they were stood there willing the little Boy Scout to flash into life and invite them over.

And then the lights changed, just as the two of us were getting down to them, Bob and me, and they were gone, immersed in whatever it is that ten hours of acquaintance gives you to talk about. Without so much as a cursory backward glance. Was that the Exocet again? Or rather a determination of his to keep a little distance between us, the working out of a little antipathy, something personal? And then, as soon as they'd made it over, he turned them right, towards Conybere Street, rather than the left that would have taken them on to Belgrave Middleway and straight down to the junction. His first mistake of the evening, I thought; racing off in front to assert his leadership, and he doesn't even know the way down there.

I let them go. The jury was still out over us, evidently, Kwesi and me, and I had no particular interest in progressing his CV for him. The tower blocks were on the cusp of losing their blushing innocence, and turning the used, sink-estate pallor of not-so-whitewash. But still it felt good to be leant up against the railings, watching it all drain to sepia as the skyline reverted to its default, decaying, gap-toothed grin. Bob stayed, too, to share it for a minute or so, slumped on the railings in an affectation of disinterest that is his way, before telling me that he'd see me down there. As he walked off in Kwesi's footsteps, I found myself shaking the spiky hands of the convicts, rubbing their blotched leaves and the incongruously delicate stems with their savage spikes. They bit down into the pads of my cold fingers, bit down harder than I'd imagined they could, began to make them sing. Just like they'd be singing for the next few hours, I thought, as they fished in and out of the pockets and purses of all those unfortunate passers-by.

It wasn't a protest or anything, my staying put. Just me availing myself of an excuse that had presented itself, to wait on that glorious dying of the light while they waited a little on me. Bob, I was sure, wouldn't mind waiting. And it's not like I hung around there that long. Just allowed them a couple of minutes, before my recalcitrant feet headed off after them, off down Conybere, because I didn't see the point of beating him.

It's not such a long street, about five hundred yards I suppose, straight as a die until the last hundred or so, where it kicks back a little and round. There was no sign of them as I started to come down; I wondered whether they could possibly have already made it over that four hundred yards to the kick-back. Or maybe they'd just slipped over on to one of the streets that run parallel, on to one of the girls, Emily or Angelina, both of them ersatz little distractions that will rush you nowhere in particular. Surely even he couldn't have taken them that far off course. I stuck with Conybere, as much because I usually do anyway. I learned long ago that it's any way but the

Middleway, but Conybere's one of the more interesting runs in; the soulless builds of social housing don't do much for me, but the odd vestige of an industrial heyday occasionally shows through, like the previous text of a badly scraped palimpsest. And great swathes of unloved green reclaimed from the chain-makers and riveters, but then abandoned and consigned to an indolent present, nothing to do but entertain the joyriders around here, and petty arsonists. Towards the bottom, down by where it leans back on itself, the trees of the regeneration have grown and filled out and matured, and now manage to soften the imperious gaggle of inner city multi- storeys that form up into its horizon.

By far the most imposing thing along here is St. Albans, sitting about halfway down; it has a massiveness of red brick bulk that presses itself tight up against the pavement, intimidating almost, as though it were trying to strong-arm you into the place. The tower at the west end shoots up must be sixty, eighty feet, like an elevator, a hotline to the Lord. Like a Watchtower. It's got a bold Victorian self-confidence to it, built to project a muscular, assertive Christianity, a go out into the benighted world and take unto them the Hope of the Lord. But the passing of the years and the shift in the social palate have emasculated it somewhat, and it has been besieged on two sides by a 70s' council estate, and a modern primary school on the third. Slowly being devoured by its originating preoccupations. But on its eastern front it's kept a dozen or so alms-houses that it hugs close to itself, Victorian too, obviously, all corbels and civic swagger, high roofs that do their best to screen out the leering upper floors of adjacent tower blocks, hugs them close in an attempt to maintain some vestige of dignity. As though determined to keep the glam-rock urban renewal at arm's length. A line in the sand.

I took a fancy to it when I started passing it in the mornings, took a liking to its ballsy will to live, and Googled it, to colour my walking time. It's a Pearson Church, from 1881. Nine years, it took, from its being completed to its consecration. Nine years – almost a decade in which the congregation railed against the High Church services that the vicar tried to introduce, a fiercely Protestant flock balking at an Anglo-Catholic Lamb of God. I didn't know any of this, before my ambulant conversion. Drove by it dozens of times, completely ignorant of quite how eloquently all that Victorian propriety, those firm lines and fine upstanding supporting ribs and crisp geometric balance could speak of the heightened sentiment that had played itself out around here a hundred years ago. And that it could be induced to tell of it quite so loquaciously. The Reverend Pollock – James Samuel Pollock – who for a time had needed a police escort to take him back and forth, to and from the place, that he might conduct his less than welcome services. Though they welcomed him in, eventually, and he ended up being sufficiently acceptable to have gotten himself a blue granite Celtic Cross, in the yard, after giving thirty or so years and the greater part of his spirit to his take on the Lord. When you're stopped here now, looking over the extended arms of that cross into the church, over the pews and then at the pulpit, and just try to imagine yourself situated in it all, in the protests and murmurings, the little huddles of the aggrieved and the traditions and sensibilities and consciences that drove them on, how fundamental it was to who they considered themselves to be, you cannot but wonder, And for what? Look around at the inheritance, the legacy, the outworking of all that passion, all that worry. Look at the *terroir* around here, its Christianlessness, and it seems nothing more than a snub to them. They protested for an entire decade, and just nine, ten decades on, this entire Christian edifice appears to be hanging on here by nothing more than a tenacity of will stretched before ineluctable odds. Which is, perhaps, a definition of faith, but the disjunction seems so bathetic. Stood now before it all, it's difficult to conceive of anything like a sustained Christian faith around here. Never mind an anti-Anglo-Catholicism. And certainly very little that's 'High'. -way robbery, maybe? Flats? Kids? It's just so sudden. But what really shocked me was not that it was so easy to stumble on it, this grandiose social barometer, but that for the years of my drive-by, it was so easy to miss.

Carry on down to the bottom, where Conybere meets Gooch Street, and there's a sign at the junction, an imposing cast-iron arch made by CP Belcher. Whenever I pass by it I always try and make time here, stop and with my fingers trace its wide arc up as far as five-nine will allow, playing them over the filigree lettering as though I'm taking a brass rubbing. It has always looked to me like the top jaw of an opening shark's mouth moving in to swallow something prey-like, the lower half already buried into the flesh of the landscape. While the River Rea gurgles somewhere below, unseen, sounding like a blood-letting or a throttling. The Beorma arch, it's called. Birmingham: the hamlet of the followers of Beorma, who came by, c.700, and took a liking to the place. Pushing in, probably up along the Tame Valley from what is now Tamworth-way. Before whom there was ... what? What, and where, is Birminghame? The Anglo-Saxon 'migration', it's known as, which seems a somewhat casual euphemism to describe a couple of hundred years of ethnic blood- letting, of Anglo-Saxon martial virility. *I am at one with fire, at play with the wind, spun about with glory, restless for the road ahead. I am a smoking coal, consumed with burning. Comrades very often lay me across their hands that the proud may kiss me. Then I raise myself up and they bow down to me in their multitudes.* I got to read someone, recently, disputing from the safety of his ivory tower the generally accepted narrative of a Saxon 'cleansing', to put forward what was for him the more palatable idea of the Saxons as a cultural elite, one that merely demanded the vanquished Britons defer to them, and maybe then allowed them a little light emulation, a little reflected gangsta-swagger. Allowed them to ape English. They called the Britons – the indigenes – they called them *wealhish*. Which meant 'foreigners'. And then, as they conquered them, 'slaves'. *Wealhish*, from which, Welsh. They called them foreigners. *Bow down to me in your multitudes.*

They'd long gone by the time I got down there, Kwesi and his flock, gone completely, off radar. I wondered whether they had missed this one as well, as they'd passed it, this elegant gravestone to the multiple appropriations of which we inadvertently seem to be a part or to which we are witness. Rushing by with their helmets and buckets and indifference, down to Bristol Street. But I've always been slow to take my leave from it. It all so nearly passed me by, as I passed by this way, quarantined in the comfort of my car. And only when I'd been forced out did I get to see something of these lives up close, the soaring glories and the grubby little hatefulness. I love this shark, have loved it from the moment I discovered it gorging on Highgate. The glory of history red in tooth, and all that. A bald, unreflective celebration of the arrival of the proto-English. But of course that's what it's always been about, Birmingham – City of a Thousand Raids.

But did he know, is what I'm really wondering as my fingers once more play over the proud lettering, and the plaintive soundtrack fills my ears – did he really know, after only one day, to turn them right instead of that so more obvious left?

*

When I finally made it down there Bob was sort of in situ, a good twenty yards off the lights, alternately dragging on a smoke and flipping one of the coins he'd already gathered. Of course he hadn't started soliciting yet; his helmet was on the pavement, leant in to the railings just the way he was, so presumably someone had tossed something in on their way past. Taking pity, perhaps. Or the piss, given that it looked like it was a ten pence piece. I couldn't imagine us comparing the takings this year anyway, but even so; typical of him, the cheeky twat, to have made a point of getting himself in front, just in case. He had his collar pulled up against the dropping temperature, and in his longish fire tunic, and with his fag and his insouciant coin-tossing manner, he was doing a passable impression of something noir. In little more than a Blues T-shirt and a NATO pullover, my impression was of a tiresome evening lying ahead, tiresome and cold. As I got to him, and leaned in to the railings next to him, Janus-like, a parody of a love-chaired couple, I suddenly found myself having to fight the urge to purloin one of his smokes and light up, too. I don't think for the Bogart effect; just to kill a little time, maybe, and forge a little bit of a connexion, some sort of unanimity in the face of having to kick this thing off.

I had been right about our having to share the pickings, though. I'd caught sight of her as I'd made my way down Bristol Street, looking as I was for anything resembling a distraction. Anything other than the prefabrication of concrete offices that rear up against the pavement back there, their bald austerity a disdainful finger not only to the Victorian embellishment of Wrentham Street, twenty yards away, but to sensibility in general. Someone had thought to pebbledash the frontage, and it's now a mass of tiny hollows and crevices wherein thirty years of soot, carbon and city grime have accumulated to give the sheer walls a fittingly close-to-death-grey pallor. So I was almost pleased to make her out, I suppose, one of the stalwart charioteers from this morning, still there in the thick of it, pacing around, brandishing her leather, pleased that I had something alive to look upon. Though somehow they'd all seemed bigger earlier, more significant, more of an imposition. I don't know, maybe the dusk had diminished her. Whatever; she certainly didn't seem to portend vanquishment and slavery, just something approaching bathos. There was a worn air to her, a world-weariness as she padded around like a clichéd pastiche of fin-de-siècle poverty. The shawled head-covering that all but obscured her face, the layers of thick wool, the heavy cotton skirt dropping away to her ankles, gently swinging to and fro as she moved between the cars, a slow sashaying to the measured, a-rhythmic beat of her footstep. Even as I got to where Bob was leaned, I still couldn't make out for sure how old she might be, what with the fading light and still a little distance between us, whether that used look about her, that steady deliberation in her step was down to her age or just the collateral of a penchant for Tzuica. Or is it Raki over there? Or meths? A plodding Transylvanian incarnation of The Grim Reaper, I'd thought, an especially impoverished Reaper, on the lookout for averted, vulnerable eyes as she passed between and selected from the purgatoried. While the damned, behind their firmly closed windows, were all of them intent on just hunkering down.

'To do that for a fucking crust.' He pulled on his fag, long and hard, his cheeks disappearing like San Fran in an earthquake.

'Bobby boy, you're doing it for a charity ...'

'No, I'm *supposed* to be doing it ... '

I turned, both of us facing east now, into the wind that had begun to flex itself, and watched the tip of his Silk Cut fire up again in a parody of the red lights that were holding back all of that traffic from which we still weren't collecting. And then, gesturing across to the other side of the junction behind us, he exhaled a thin stream of blue smoke from between tightly pursed lips. Over on the into-city carriageway, OJ and a couple of the others were dipping in and out of the traffic, cajoling and entertaining like a troupe of street performers. Believing. 'Jesus, if that's what they're expecting ...'

I wondered whether she might have a little something warm about her, something that she would use to take the edge off their apathy, and whether she'd be up for exchanging a drag on it for one of Bob's fags. Watching her stoic progress through the traffic, it was impossible not to be impressed by her quiet dignity, by how she managed to maintain something approaching self-respect. How exactly do you pull that off, the wandering around stationary cars for an entire day with a bucket, begging from the indifferent, from the antipathetic, and still be able to hold their eye at the end of it? Assuming they even bother to look at you. I doubted her takings would be impairing ours, if and when we decided to start the taking.

'Give it an hour, then we'll see how it stands. A quick hour, and then to some pub somewhere?' Though I knew that was a lie; this was going to be anything but quick. 'Yeah?' I simply couldn't stay put any longer. My standing there – my having the option to stand there – just seemed to be a mockery of her. Rather desultorily, I eased my back from the railings and headed off along the thin strip of reservation between the carriageways, in towards town. Twenty or thirty yards, that'd be enough, surely, and then start back towards the lights. As I moved off, I found my hands rolling the helmet back and forth, in lieu of that cigarette I suppose, occasionally spinning it up a foot or so as though it were a basketball or something. Something other than a pot in which to be carrying off their cash. Is that what I was trying to project to them, subconsciously, a huddled-to-me, don't-really-want-to-be-involved-in-any-of-this bright yellow barrier? A Ying to Kwesi's Yang?

I'd got no more than halfway into my twenty yards and suddenly there was a hand reached out of a window, in its pursed fingers a clutch of silver aimed at scuppering my cunning ploy. Quickly followed by a head with a pretty little smile that was doing its best to disguise the tiredness of the face, and lustrous ice-blue eyes that I would like to have seen first thing this morning, before eight or nine hours in front of a computer screen had had their way with them. And then, 'Hiya. Good for ya, you boys.' Her tone, too, all irrepressible bouncy animation, seemed completely disconnected from the day that her face suggested. Is this the Wogan effect? Has a disfigured Bear succeeded in sparking some enthusiasm here? Maybe I just needed to get on board.

'Oh, errr, thanks. Yeah ... sorry to be fiddling with your journey home, but thanks anyway. Sure there'll be some kid somewhere who'll love you for it.'

She leaned herself back into the car, and I took the fact of her continuing to explain as an invitation to follow her in there. 'That's all of my change. So it's self-preservation, really. I can't be pressured in to a dirty-rag windscreen wash, now, can I?' By then I was leant on the door, as good as parallel for the last few words, and this close up I decided that that striking icy blueness was in fact steeled by something like detachment, by what I thought might even be a vague capacity for cruelty, and it was equal parts intimidating and alluring. She held my eye for more than a moment, gauging my reaction to her reaction, and then looked away, straight ahead to where there was evidently still Reaping to be done. I didn't follow her gaze; rather my eyes dropped briefly on to her hemline, a short workaday business pinstripe that cut across her legs a good four or five inches above the knee. Her feet were back, off the pedals and rested on the mat in the footwell so that her legs were lifted slightly, just clear of the seat, and it gave them a tensed, trimmed definition. I thought she'd be distracting to have working alongside.

'Yeah? Good move, I suppose. Though maybe I should be sympathizing with her. Solidarity, and all that. The communion of beggars.'

'Mmmm ...' This time the stare was accompanied by a nod, the implication obviously being that this time my gaze ought to be following hers. 'Looks like she could do with a little of your solidarity about now.' It was frayed, ever so slightly, little charcoal-grey and white fingers of hemline resting on her thigh.

She was there, about a dozen cars in front and to the left, stood alongside the windscreen of a grubby white van that was pulled up on the inside lane, waiting to turn up past the mosque. The guy driving it was raging at her, his head and shoulders fully out of the window, his purpling, barely controlled fury inches from her face, now that the shawl had been pulled back a little, in spite of the cold. I half expected to see a fist describing an arc at any moment. Quite sobering, I'd thought, that there could be that sort of emotion simmering just below all of this inertia. Obviously, she was in need of some practice with assessing the victim-ness of eyes. And yet there was that dignity again; she was completely unperturbed by him, didn't concede so much as a blink. It was something beyond even indifference. More like transcendence. The whole thing was completely surreal.

'Wow. Now that's a man. A man in touch with his inner man. Over ... what, a quid?' The higher pitch of a few of the 'fucks' travelled back through the noise of engines ticking over. 'Hope he doesn't give himself a coronary or anything. Despite the job description, my grasp of CPR is pretty tenuous at the best of times.'

'No. No, not at all. I'm with angry man all the way. Last thing I need after a day like I've had is to have to come up with excuses why I don't want or can't have my window smeared with yesterday's bloody bog water. And then have her pretending she doesn't know what 'no' is as she does it anyway.'

'*Okaay* ... wow. Again. Maybe you could learn Slavic for 'green card?'? Do we do green cards?'

'Wish we did a few more green lights. So I wouldn't have to put up with the bitch.'

And then, as if to excuse me from having to come up with something else conciliatory, the lights changed to her wished-for green, and ol' blue eyes could be off and angry man didn't have to punch anyone. I made for Bob and the central reservation. He hadn't moved, hadn't even finished his fag; during the performance I'd noticed him still leant back on the railings, watching it all, the whole duet, with a look of detached interest. I was glad I'd stayed there with him earlier, coveting his addiction for as long as I had when I'd first gotten down there. Had I been even a little bit tainted by OJ's enthusiasms, been just a couple of minutes more eager, and it could have been me dangling my charity in an angry man's face. Though, given that I hadn't really been doing much in the way of helmet-waving, probably not.

Is it a rage they're all a party to now? And it's nothing but what is always thought to be the fiction of Good Old English Reserve that keeps most of them from climbing out of windows? I'd loved that steely stoicism of hers, and thought how well it would have served me in the days when that early morning numbness of mine was under daily assault. But bloody hell, did it seem to push people's buttons.

'Can you feel it, Bobby Boy, all that anger? I'd be surprised if they'll be giving anything to anybody tonight.'

'Nah, you'll be pulling in more than ever, now. Just follow far enough in her wake and by the time you get to them, they'll be feeling guilty as fuck and shoving cash at you. She could even be a part of our pincer. This is going to be like taking candy from a Romanian baby.'

'I can't see that angry twat feeling the need to be shriven.'

'We pulled in ... what, seventy quid between us last year? A beer says we get the better of it.'

'I don't get it. These lot were dropping in fivers and tenners last year, some of them, and they must have known that most of it would be going out to the four corners – horns in Africa and tinpot orphanages in Eastern Europe and all the rest of it. Barely one of them gave us the knock-back. And yet, when some bag of a basket case is stood there right in front of them, first hand in all her gory, they just blow her away, every last one of them, and there's not the slightest awareness of the disconnect between the two acts. I don't get the schizophrenic mind-set, quite how the charity can co-exist with such indifference, with all that contempt.'

'It's our love of due process, mate. Give twenty quid to a quango, and every last penny of it will have to be accounted for, every brass tack. Makes it seem legit, even though most of it'll get siphoned off long before it reaches any needy little fuck. When she's stood in front of you, there's always the feeling that within ten minutes of your giving it to her, your fiver will be petrol in the tank of some nice new Beamer she'll have got parked up round the corner. Feels like you're being fucked over. She makes Johns out of them.'

'That's bollocks. They can't possibly think that she's out here doing it 'cos it's an easy ride.'

'She's a fucking fraud.'

'She's a busted up old cunt out on an icy November evening! Her hands are in and out of a bucket of freezing water, being told to piss off when she's not being ignored totally. I'm wandering around here with a fluorescent jerkin and all the comfort of my apathy, and by your reckoning my half-arsed cup will twice over-floweth hers by the end of the night.'

'And just think how pleased OJ will be with the spillage of your cup.'

'Nah.' The lights had changed once more and were bringing it all back down to a stop. My fingers had started to feel thick and clumsy with the cold, and so I stood myself off the railings and began rolling the helmet around again, tossing my couple of quid of loose change. 'I just can't see it. How they can so easily reconcile all that generosity with such parsimony of spirit.' I'd noticed her shuffling back out there, the moment it'd all come to a halt, pushing off the railings with her slops bucket and chamois. I eased myself forward into it, too, as much because I was starting to feel like a prick again, just staying back there fondling a helmet, what with being all dressed up for action. 'I just cannot get my head around it, that sort of casual, impromptu anger.' The sun was by now fading on us quite quickly, slipping behind the office blocks and towers of Five Ways. As I stepped down off the curb, I caught her eye despite the now half-hearted efforts of her shawl and the dusk, and gave her a nod, a little handshake of esprit de corps.

I can see her now, as though she were in front of me now, stood not more than ten yards away. Paused by another van, though the window of this one remained tightly wound up. She'd hesitated before it this time, maybe because she'd got the other bloke's eyes so massively, so publicly wrong. As our eyes met her hand had been moving down into the bucket, as though on auto, but at that moment she stopped it dead. Stopped her begging dead to slowly, deliberately, almost theatrically lift her hand from out of the bucket, and gave me the finger. Staring levelly at me, as quietly hostile as though it had been me hanging out of a window earlier, had been my purpling face pressed up against hers. Her lips pursed in to something like the beginnings of an 'F...', and it wasn't too hard to infer the silent 'you'. I managed to hold her stare for about two seconds, in shock as much as anything, just to see whether there must surely have been a misunderstanding, another angry man somewhere behind me, and then I just had to look away. She kept it up and out there for must have been ten, twenty awkward seconds. Nonplussed, yes, certainly a little embarrassed, but it was anger that I was feeling – I thought of ol' ice-blue eyes – so fucking angry that I'd actually been sucked in, had allowed myself to be co-opted out into a freezing evening to collect for ingrates like her. The cheeky *bitch*.

I turned away again, back into the traffic. They'd all been privy to it, of course. Caught up in the caprice of the red lights, they'd had nothing to do but watch our little street show, and every pair of eyes within range would have been upon us. Usually, for all their material generosity, it's pretty rare to actually catch someone's eye down here, unless maybe you're dressed up as a big green traffic light. But tonight, as I tried to make as dignified a withdrawal as I thought possible, I couldn't look anywhere and not have a thanks-for-the-distraction pair of eyes staring back at me. Almost automatically, I went for the safety of my helmet. The coins made a satisfying deep jingling as I flipped them again, tumbling around the echo-chamber that was the bottom of the helmet, and when I sent them up, the spinning silver became a glistening thread describing some sort of thrusting arc, and then they hung suspended for a moment, caught in the juxtaposition of the dusk and the fluorescence of the street lights that had just burst into life above, before collapsing back down. Little shards of pure, winking brilliance. It was distraction enough to get me out of the gridlock and off the carriageway, I reckoned, to the neutral ground of the railings. Over to the indifference of Bob. Two hours, maybe, to get through, and I reckoned sat on a fence was as good a way as any to get through them.

Almost at the curb, I gave it another tinkle, but it *still* felt like a guilty weight, for God's sake, and I couldn't figure why. Because I'm out here against my will, unbelieving? Because of Romanian babies? It's as though she's done one over on *me*, like *I'm* the one being pincered, pinned between ungrateful dead like her and Kwesi and his CV. He'd still be over there, of course, with his unbearable enthusiasm. I imagined him looking across, tut-tutting at what he'd no doubt characterise as my defeatism, my failure; *enthusiasm is infectious*. Well, I've got the beginnings of a fiver in here, Bunny, and fuck you …

I suppose that my glistening thread would have been at something like its apex when I heard him, the past calling out. The long buried timbre of his voice caught me so unawares that I mistimed the collect and silver rang out on the tarmac, a sharp, bright accompaniment to the last two of his syllables:

'Pig. Pig Jennings.' I hadn't heard it for years, and despite the risk of rows and rows of schadenfreude that I'd been intent on avoiding of course I turned round. They were eager eyes, not just mildly amused like most of the others, but eager to be recognized, abetted by a slightly mischievous grin.

The guy reached forward and unconsciously I found myself moving towards him with a helmet outstretched, and the tinkling sounded out once again. 'Piggy Dave Jennings, a fireman. A fireman! Who'd have thought?' The voice is from way back, and the face, too, is vaguely familiar, though I'm having to strip out all the accretions that testosterone has layered on to his physiology, having to pare back the strengthening around the chin and thickening of the jawline, all the hormonal meatier-ness, the manliness. The nose is proud, would probably have been proud from way back whenever. But those eyes, those bloody eyes, touch buttons somewhere. They come from somewhere in an intimately shared past, a couple of plaintive, lustrous mulatto coals staring out at me. I remember them as pleading, somehow, as vulnerable. 'You haven't got the faintest idea who I am, have you?' From the cacophony of horns starting up behind I'm assuming that the lights must have changed again but he's steady, confident, putting it in first but holding the clutch, and his smile widens. He reaches over to take the edge of my helmet, and shakes it gently. 'I always did have you down as a do-gooder. Though I suppose you didn't have much choice, really, did you? All things considered.' But eventually the horns become too much and he lifts the clutch, and I watch him, I watch the back of Carlos' head disappearing down the Bristol Road.

3

The Brewer and Baker juts out into the traffic on a bleak promontory of Highgate, a tarmac-grey finger pointing away down the Stratford Road. Hemmed in as it is by two of the city's busiest trunk roads, it doesn't strike you as a natural stopping-off point, as being especially well positioned for pulling in passing trade. Or maybe it's actually a crooked finger, and in fact it is beckoning rather than directing. Either way, it was Kwesi, of all people, who'd pulled us in. Let's not mention that it had taken him until almost nine to do it, to have finally given up on goading everyone with that Goddamn enthusiasm of his. Most of us were by then pretty much wilted; for at least the last hour, I'd kept it going only on the back of a few of the succouring verses that I'd managed to dredge up from somewhere: 'Go and sell that thou hast, and give to the poor, and thou shalt have treasure in heaven.' That type of stuff. Pithy little mantras, the truth of which I was no longer sure I had any faith in. I wondered whether, on the Lord's reward card system, there might perhaps be a dispensation, a double reckoning, for those who sell, and give, and yet no longer entirely believe, either in the heaven bit, or even in the giving, now, after that bitch and her finger.

Three hours: I'd reckoned on Pudsey having had his pound of flesh. The lack of light was anyway making waving helmets at passing traffic more likely to end up in donations of organs than of money. And of course, OJ had to be conscious of his Health and Safety remit. Ultimately, it was his call, which unfortunately left us reliant upon the man and his manic sense of purpose to bring it to an end. But then suddenly he's announcing that he's had enough and is all for heading for the pub. As though someone had brushed up against an on-off switch, turned his ice-water into wine. Aahhh, OJ; perhaps it was relief, but out of that blue I found myself taking to the new boy, forgiving him his reputation, the accretion of those rumours, the ruin of my morning. Though his decision to point us all pub-ward was a surprise; I wouldn't have had him down as a drinker, or certainly not an inner-city beer-and-scratchings man, down with us lot. Maybe that's why we were here, why he chose this place when there were much closer pubs, most of them with a little more history and all of them with a lot more character. Pile everyone into the least salubrious place you can think of, and nobody's going to be particularly inclined to stay for more than the one. But it was taking-the-piss cold out there, even for November, so I wasn't going to argue, was I? I knew it was likely to be warm, it was close to the station, there'd be beer.

But even with the prospect of putting this thing out of its misery with a few jars, I couldn't shake my sense of foreboding on the way up. I like a drink, at least as much as the next guy, but even I'm a little picky about where I settle down to do it. I'd spent my formative years under the tutelage of Seth Armstrong and Annie Walker, and it was that kind of generally benevolent, comforting alcoholarchy that I'd managed to carry in to adulthood, even if lately it had entailed an avoidance of mirrors in late night toilets. And though I'd never before stepped foot in the Brewer – I doubt that any of us would have – I was pretty sure that it wouldn't be the kind of venue to reinforce those gentle conceptions of mine. It isn't rocket science, is it, after all? It cannot be more than a hundred yards, door to door, from the pub to the Trinity Centre. The Trinity Centre, formerly Holy Trinity Church, which we have to inspect twice a year to make sure they're not sleeping in the fire exits or pawning the fire extinguishers. It was built in the nineteenth century, its design seemingly intended to remind its congregants of the austerity of God's love, of exactly how demanding were His precepts. It lours, still, over the Digbeth skyline, its turrets prodding belligerently at the heavens. And yet it, too, must have been touched by Christ's Caritas somewhere along the line, by the lure of heavenly treasure, because in the 70s it became the transubstantiation of word into deed and turned itself into a homeless centre, and there must now be two hundred or so blokes that have no other calling it home. Its tough love nevertheless a respite from society's disdain. And I reckon – because this is still our patch, remember, and as we drive past here on out-duties we see the disdained gathering around the open-at-eleven doors – that most of them are going to be willing to risk that hundred-odd yards of societal opprobrium to get themselves a drink there. It's probably considered a short sprint, in relation to the ponderous journey of a shitty life. Apparently I should envy them their daily lot, because by dint of it they get first dibs at the kingdom.

Whatever. Having briskly walked the half-mile up here, we weren't about to start being prissy when the temperature was down to something like minus two: as soon as we got to the door, the chill pretty much grabbed us by our pulled up collars, an inversion of an officious bouncer, and threw us across the threshold. What met us was the single square room that constitutes the place; save a lonely corridor off, presumably to what passes for toilets, that was to be the evening's deal. Four walls and a low-slung suspended ceiling. It's that bluntly matter-of-fact: what hit me the moment I stepped in was the absence of things, of any of the normal paraphernalia that works to civilise a pub's primary function. It felt looted, stripped of any sort of pretence of 'going out'. No pictures, no trinkets, not even a token horse brass. The only distraction in the place lay in the faces of the patrons – the once-whiteness of the eyes and the bloody lattice-work of the cheeks and the skin's slurry relationship with its skeletal substrate – and in their intense concern with the matter in hand. We'd invited ourselves in to the living room of the dispossessed and the thwarted, and it was stale and unloved and smelled of nothing so much as ... no, not of piss, but of *pissed*, the constantly, perennially pissed: the odour of a defeated people. The faint taste of it mingled with the rich taste of blood in the back of my throat, a hard walk on a cold night, and I took a minute to swallow them down. And then shivered: it seemed warm after the cold of outside. I suppose I was reassuring myself that it would be alright in here – it *is* a pretty good rejoinder, putting yourself out of it, making yourself insensible when it's anyway indifference all around. Maybe 'Brewer and Baker' should be the collective noun for disappointed lives: a 'Brewer' of winos. It was humming, almost, the whole room, with something like the anticipatory buzz that you get in an exam room just before the call for quiet; you sensed a dread of the sound of the bell.

We weren't the only ones in there – as in we weren't the only fire brigade. I noticed a couple of familiar faces on the way through, little groups of erstwhile collectors who weren't quite as possessed of Kwesi's serendipitous stamina, evidently, and who knew when to finish their bucket-waving. A pretty good indication that it hadn't been an impromptu decision of his, this Brewer finale, but then I didn't really think he would do spur of the moment. Gemma had made it up here, against her travelling-home odds, and I'd traded a nod and a grin for a flash of her smile as I'd come past. Even in here, you couldn't but be beguiled by her, by the infectiousness of one of her hellos, by that sparkle. Like a couple of the others, she was still in uniform, the plain black trousers and the anaemic blue of the shirt. Flashes of black epaulette at the shoulder. Her shoes had condensed the strip lights down to a needle point on each of their plastic toecaps, little diamonds set on cushions of parade gloss. And there was even a tie, still, now, at nine o'clock, done up to the collar. It does no one any favours, our chronically unflattering uniform, and it never ceases to amaze me that people wear it out when they have a choice. But somehow Gem manages to carry its stultifying blandness as though it were an intentional sartorial affront, a deliberate reproach to aesthetics. Her trousers are a cut too small for her, and hitched a little too high, and the hem lifts off and away from the shine of her shoes. Above its trim beltline her shirt just billows and balloons randomly, its jaded blue tails barely tucked in, the lie of the fabric barely disturbed by the flatness of her chest: no shape, no definition, nothing like a pucker or a crease gathered around a nipple. Just leaves herself out there as a big, blue, androgynous target, as though there were no point.

We sent Benny to the bar, while the rest of us – me, and Bob, of course, and somehow Nigel too – triangulated ourselves almost reflexively into a huddle. A defensive little redoubt, but against what exactly? There hadn't been any aggression, it wasn't especially loud in the place, or raucous, or overtly any more threatening than any other unfamiliar pub. No knuckle-dragging, unblinking thug up a corner, a cliché of territorial cock strut. I'm not sure the others were even that bothered. Maybe it was just me working myself up off a bleak imagination, tapping into a few easy certainties. But where is the fail-safe in somewhere like this, I was thinking, the something to lose? A Trinity Centerian buries glass into someone's face, and how is his life going to be so different from there on in? There's no reason to hold back if it all kicks off. With no house left to lose, no missus, no kids – an acute absence, even a denial, of all those civilising concerns – why would that anyone feel the need to stop punching. Especially if it is one of society's disdainful that he's punching. If it were to kick off.

Benny was still at the bar, his interloper's booming baritone now competing with one of the disdained, an avuncular bundle of a regular, Brian Blessed - beard and all. Both of them were leaned in to the counter's cheap melamine, their faces inches from one another, their guffawing laughter probably the loudest noise in there. Stood next to them, barely any space between them, there was another guy, all done up in an albeit now shabby two-piece, collar and tie, patent leathers that would have cut it a few years back. Leaned forward too, but away from Benny and Brian and in to his own buddy. I watched, mesmerized by him: this guy was raging at his mate, or rather in the direction of his mate, his contorted face a mosaic of glowing reds and purples projecting forward, his body quivering almost involuntarily. Little strings of spittle forming, which would occasionally break free and gob their way over the short space that separated them, and land on his buddy's jacket, pint, face. And this other bloke was completely calm, equable, beatific almost, just nodding quietly in the face of this onslaught.

From away back he was fascinating, with the once fineness of his clothing conjuring whatever back story, the placid sufferance of his mate. But I couldn't have stood there, where Benny was, so close to him, so indifferent, so comfortable. He'd noticed him, of course, Benny, even though the anger itself was contained entirely within the bloke's demesne, pushing out no further than an inch or two. Yet there he stayed, leant in to the Beard, bouncing off his new best friend, and no more than a lazy eye out for the mania to his right. But of course he would fit in here, being possessed of the off-key, kooky world view that I suppose is pretty much a given in the place. And a facility with people, an empathy. I like Benny; he took me under his wing when I first joined the watch, when most of the others seemed little more than indifferent – perhaps I don't appreciate how close I came to being a regular in here myself. And in here, in the Brewer, he's finding good company in what for me is an uncomfortable space. I still couldn't take my eyes from him and his outrage; I wondered if it was a learned skill, emoting like that in public, being able to keep it so close, whether he'd developed it over time in response to being barred or beaten. And for how long must he have been doing it in here for them to be paying him not the slightest bit of attention?

'I think' – Benny, having made it back from the bar – 'he's just realised how bad the beer is in here.' But I didn't much care, now I had some, as to the provenance of what I was about to knock back, or suddenly to the entertainment up at the bar any more. I now had something in my hands, and we were off the streets, and there wasn't anything like a bucket-rattle anywhere within earshot. I lifted a glass to him, to his ease, his gregariousness. His indifference to people's sensibilities, the way he sails up to and often over the line, and just carries it off with a grin of sassy bonhomie. A couple of times I've been out drinking with him, and watched enviously from his slipstream how easily and confidently he hooks up with people. He has people laughing, even as he riles them. Women, I know from experience, often find themselves laughing.

But the Brewer doesn't really do women. And so, inevitably, having been on a little circuit around the room, our collective attention was always going where it was going.

After a couple of false starts it settled predictably enough on to the new boy, on to OJ. Why would it not? Any change in gaffer is going to kick up some interest. What's he like? Is he really as bad as they made out? I looked at him working the room. On the back of a big take – it had been a big take, and a big take is always going to reflect well on a gaffer, whether he's new or not – he was slipping himself confidently into and out of the various little Fire Brigade groupings, balancing an easy familiarity with that always present supervisory role. He has gravitas. I was still shocked that, give or take a little hyperactivity, he'd made relatively few ripples, had been less the troublesome diva than that reputation of his had prepared us against. I don't know, maybe he's a slow starter. But I still couldn't fathom why he'd have chosen this place for a drink: he seemed as out of it as the rest of us. Maybe it was his way of continuing the charity thing: having decided that today was to be a day of charity, he would therefore be on it *for* the day, because completely immersing himself in whatever is exactly the type of thing you'd expect of him. Dragging the rest of us along with him, that we might see and believe. For a minute or so I stood looking over at him, wrestling with my agnosticism, for some unknown reason finding myself focusing on his lips as they formed his words for him, powerful lips, muscular, prehensile. They seemed to catch a hold of each phonation as it came through, and rolled with it, toying with it playfully before allowing it to continue, sending it out on a smirk. And then, as he hove over, I started to pick up on a Fire Brigade word here and there, the odd half sentence. Inevitable, I suppose; after only a day, what else would he have to talk to us about? But it turned me off, and so I tuned back in to the comfort of my little huddle: '... someone keeps sticking niggers through my letterbox ...'

He figured to get away with it, evidently, despite us being geographically where we were, right in the middle of the rigorous cosmopolitanism of Highgate – though the only colour I'd seen in any of the faces in here was the gorgeous purple flush that comes of well-practised drinking. Except, of course, in Kwesi's. '... niggers, through the letterbox.' I watched as he moved on again, fully into view now, and possibly into earshot. 'I think I'm being blackmailed.'

Does it make a difference? Does joking about it, even when they're shitty little jokes like that, affect your perception, altering slightly and subliminally the way that you act and react and relate to people? 'Irish bloke goes to the doctor's, complaining of an orange cock. Doc asks him what he does. "I eat Wotsits all day and watch porn."' And so every Irish bloke you meet thereafter is tainted, becomes slightly more a doppelganger of the indolent twat pulling himself off in a corner of your subconscious? I have to admit that I did eventually smile at the 'serendipitous' quip, thought it was quite tight as a piss-take because of the implied baggage. Which, of course, necessitates a recognition *of* the baggage. But I suppose I liked it because it was so avowedly anti PC, a bald transgressive statement against the imposition of a politic. Baldly speaking untruth to power, it would seem after today. But the transgression still sanctified it. Though I would never have laughed at it, not out loud. Not in a thousand years, not for him. He's a prick, Nigel, a poisonous little tosspot, and not only was this just lazy but now, after not that bad a day, I suppose, and a pretty ok evening in here so far, it seems unprovoked and nasty and calculated to be divisive. I turned to Benny, turned fully, bodily, pointedly: 'D'you pull in much? Anything near what you did last year?' I still wasn't sure what Benny thought of him. But for that moment, it seemed, he was happy just to lift his glass with me, and we drained them down and let some space open up. He was right, I decided, about the beer.

I sensed Nigel was out somewhere where he wasn't used to being. With what, for him, seemed like uncharacteristic self-awareness, suddenly he too was raising his glass and downing a couple of mouthfuls, a submissive mirroring, while his eyes scanned the room for something to move it on, something sacrificial. So naturally I assumed we were about to have our attention dragged back to our new friend at the bar, an obvious soft target for a little diversionary piss-taking. And then instead it came at one of us: 'I see Gemma's getting the transvestite look down to a tee.' She was still over by the door, billowing out past a couple of blokes off Red Watch. Just chatting away, animating her little gathering with that energy of hers that seems to define her, enthusing over something of nothing, probably; open, at ease, interested. Uncalled for. So I was more than a little pissed when Bob indulged him with a half-laugh, which the nob took for an offer of redemption and snatched up by electing to get the next round in. He's such a cunt. Though despite my dislike of him, I'll still take a beer off him, and just call it payment for forbearance. Why wouldn't I raise a glass of his beer to his discomfort, however fleeting it might have been?

He pushed off through the crowd towards the bar, and only then did I properly turn round to look over at Gem, to where she was still caught up in her threesome. Of course, she was completely ignorant of her complicity in his get-out – though somehow I don't think she'd have minded that much; she has the self-confidence in her, and the grace, or maybe it's hope, to have probably found and then offered the tosser some sort of olive branch. The sartorial slight certainly wouldn't have troubled her: I've seen her when she's out of the Fire Brigade disguise, out down Broad Street in a LBD that was a bold and very knowing statement of the feminine. But despite her figure, I don't think testing her with mirrors was ever a part of the Lord's grand plan. Hers is an evasive beauty: she has lustrous hair, certainly, wispy and ephemeral and gorgeous, which she wears in a bob that's just, just long enough to flirt with regulation, but her nose is hooked and raptorial, and her chin juts forward so that, together, in profile she's almost a caricature of Mr. Punch, with her quick, inquisitive eyes darting about as if looking for a Judy. As a sum of her parts, you'd think unpromising. And yet the moment she looks over again, a flirty finger separating her lips as she projects out of her group, you cannot but find yourself in love with pantomime.

I've always liked Gemma. Not everyone does, irrelevances like Nigel aside. Davey P hates her for some reason, undermines her in a real personal way that isn't at all like him, and there's a tangible edge when they're rostered together on the back of the truck. But I like her, I like her insouciance, the sanguinity, how gamey she is when everyone's taking the piss. I like the shape of her legs when she's down to shorts in the gym. And, now, I especially like the manner in which she keeps flashing that smile over this way and then playing all coquettish when I catch and hold the look. And I smile back, but of course it's a smile that's always going to be half-hearted, because work and play just don't mix. It's simpler to separate them out, adapt the First Amendment, and thereby avoid the awkwardnesses and silences and then the recriminations that inevitably follow domestic ruptures into the locker room. It happened to Dave Jones, who had to ride the rumours – which were certainties to everyone but him – with as much equanimity as he could muster, until Sam finally found compassion enough to end it to his face. What if, for instance, she were to out my peccadilloes? Her energy bowls through the late evening fug. I look at her thin wrists, with their delineated veins, and the expressive hands that move constantly to breathe life into whatever it is that she's talking about. I imagine her letting me still them. She looks over and catches me at my imagining, and smiles again.

*

'Kath' informs me that a good time is guaranteed. The cursor hovers over the contact details again. Again I deliberate.

We'd emptied out of the Brewer with the last of them, with the Disdained, after I'd managed, chain-drinking, to down about nine in anticipation of the tolling of the bell. What is it to dread last orders, to not want to be home? It's a habit I got into, in the weeks and months after Lou and I had split, when opening the front door just drove home the cold, dark aloneness. And then I took to filling the void with a beer-stocked fridge and a quickly acquired selection of strategy games, *Total War* and *Civilisation* and stuff. All of it jockeying with late night, very trashy telly. But thanks primarily to Gem and her finger, this evening I've gone for Punternet, a website that allows punters to rate and review prostitutes – although, charitable as she is, I doubt she'd find the association flattering. And the Kath-fix is pretty immediate. Just below her pretty little smile there's a review by Clit-Lic, who's something of a favourite of mine: unlike most of the work-a-day stuff that litters the site, Clit-Lic can actually write. Initially, I just liked his play on 'chick-lit', how he'd inverted the consumer / consumed relationship, but soon took to the irony and self-deprecation. His back-catalogue is time-absorbingly extensive. Tonight's is a more recent assessment:

These are good tits, slick, well-trained, and they fully deserve this ovation: I stand for them as enthusiastically as they stood for me. The nipple, almost the moment I touched it, reached out eagerly to my tongue, swelling up like Thunderbird 2, stiff and excitable, a miniature swollen hard-on. Can you do that on demand? Is that the mark of a pro pro?

I wanted mish – call me old fashioned – but she took the reins and did me cowgirl, clamping her toenails into my shins like spurs and then galloping down on me. I felt like whinnying, but thought it might sound a bit pervy. Her moans are long and raw, and she comes harder than the missus ever does – well, she takes considerably more care over the faking. And at least Kath doesn't interrupt *her* act with the transactional negotiations.

She simply emptied me. I am not ready for such a girl. Recommended.

'Good time guaranteed.' The cursor is still there, flicking like an impatient, table-drumming finger. Do I want to be a john? Could I be? '... well-trained tits ...' The cursor waits, still tapping. 'A whore is a deep ditch; and a strange woman is a narrow pit. She also lieth in wait as for a prey, and increaseth the transgressors among men'. That's not Clit-Lic, obviously; it's Proverbs 23; 27. And it's not their version, either; fundamentalists don't tend to use the King James'. I've still got JW ghosts moving round the house, in need of exorcism.

4

I used to think that it just took balls to drink in a pub on your own – especially a pub with which you were unfamiliar – nothing more or less than a steely self-possession. But I now realise that the point of pubs, maybe even exceptional ones like the Brewer yesterday, actually lies in the social nature of getting pissed. The blurring is important, of course, and very often the ducking and denying, but beer is an adjunct in this, an assist to the social. You hide, and seek succour, in the artificially induced friendship of the inebriated. Pubs are communal. Doing it on your own just demonstrates that a balance has been or is being inverted. It's an unhealthy, precipitous sign. I don't think it was intentional, her being late, some sort of ploy to drag into the public domain the fact that she thought my balance is currently undergoing an inversion. But late she definitely was, leaving me and my trio of beers to project into a pub that wasn't mine. Though I would doubt that it is hers, either. Whatever. Whoever actually does lay claim to this pub, it's a bugger to get served in here – hence the bulk-buy of beer sharing my table. That's three for me. I don't think she drinks much anymore, or at least I've a feeling that she won't be this evening, in present company, so I didn't presume.

The pub in which I'm waiting for my soon-to-be-ex wife, to discuss the spoils of divorce, is The White Swan, a glorious 1900 Lister Lea and Sons that only just managed to survive one of Birmingham's periodic spasms of self-harming. For a couple of decades, in the 60s and 70s, the councillors assumed the FORWARD of the city's coat of arms to be an executive order, some sort of instruction to try and raze every vestige of the city's hinterland. An ideological hard-on for change, the past as impediment to progress and all that. The flared corbels and trim little parapets beneath which I'd just walked, the delicate, completely otiose Barley Twist columns of stonemasonry that adorn the doorways, each of them stood up on little brick-work spindles, all this warmth of terracotta stonework hugging unto itself the early evening sun, it was all of it apparently only a planning meeting away from being road-widened. As a building it's friendly, and gets friendlier the closer you come into it, the somewhat gloomy expanses of the small-square leaded windows ceding to an informality, an invitingness. Over the doorway through which I've just walked there's a slim slip of a canopy that conjured for me a slightly cocked eyebrow, quizzical as I came in under it. And yet I've walked right past it all, all of this, must be a dozen times making my way in to work, this confection of baroque folds and wrinkles. Flourishes that, in their superfluity, seem to be a gaudy snub to all the modernist functionality, the Brutalism, that surrounds them and so nearly replaced them, but, before now, I'd never been in. Too out of the way for buses home.

The inside makes the same sort of impact, at first, when you come through; the tiles in the corridor wash up the walls, floor to high ceiling, a slightly garish confection of greens and creams, with a rolling, folding bullnose-tile tide-mark at about waist height. A precocious anticipation of the Seventies, all of it set off against the tight geometrical restraint of the thoroughly Victorian red, blue and taupe tiled floor. I heard my boots thudding on it as I came in, as though they were trying to get an echo out of the ceramic, almost as if trying to beef up my confidence as I made my way into an unfamiliar pub on my own. But of course the bar was indifferent when I opened the door on to it, entirely occupied with its own noise. I don't think a single man of them looked up as I went over and sat on the only vacant stool at the bar, and rested my feet self-consciously on the rail as I waited for something like bar-staff to appear.

Which gave me a moment to look about the place. The bar is a rich mahogany slab, its leading edge unevenly polished by years of leaning hands and elbows, patches of sebum-sheen where the mechanics of the set-up have unintentionally kettled the drinkers over time: the cash register; the troop of pumps; the positions to which the bar staff default when they're not serving and to which punters are drawn. I rubbed it, my little patch of sheen, to tap into past secreting and to add a little of my own to the mix and be a part of it. Behind and slightly obscured by the row of optics was the most luscious etched mirror from way back when, its silky gilded lettering advertising a Fuller Smith ale that probably hadn't seen the inside of a pub for half a century. But the floor hadn't made it across time; the glory of the hallway Mintons had given way in here to the functionality of what was now grubby and worn linoleum. An abstract off-yellow motif repeated itself into boredom. It all felt slightly lavatorial. And though it retained the grandeur of its plaster mouldings and coving, and an impressive if now redundant ceiling rose, all of which emphasised that Victorian height, the once white ceiling had become nothing more than a record of the smudged and smeared drifts of nicotine that the years had bequeathed it. A few generic pictures tried to break up the long run of the walls between them – stable hands and thoroughbreds, a benevolent squire, bucolic scenes of a never-here Eden – but none of them connected with the place, none of them spoke of anything but decorating apathy.

I must have had three or four minutes to take all of this in, sat there twiddling my discomfort, before she appeared at the other end of the bar. Straightening a degree or two out of my little slouch, I must have looked gratefully expectant as I caught her eye. But she'd come to a stop, suddenly chatty with one of her regulars – evidently affronted that I'd sat up quite so presumptuously. Asserting herself, the sullen cow, before finally deigning to a slow walk this way. She was a wizened Irish antitype, taciturn to the point of muteness, indulging me with not a syllable beyond the necessary: maybe she appreciates just how eloquent is her Guinness. But, however good a pint she keeps, I really couldn't be doing with her bollocks. So three, I thought, a trio of beer to see me out of here.

That was ten minutes ago, and sat at my table, now, trying to look like I'm not merely waiting for my blood-alcohol level to hit three hundred, I've had time to ponder it all. I like the balls of it, the chutzpah of an age that would build a pub so exuberant, so self-confident, and so clearly intended to add alcohol to the civic whole. I like the industrial ghosts that raise a glass with you, the Edwardian foundry workers coming across from Birchall Street with their hobnails and furnace thirst, and their sweaty, polishing hands. But the slippage into the make-do, the easy concession to the utilitarian? It isn't even up to it, the linoleum floor that lies where once would have lain a glorious expanse of intricate ceramic craftsmanship – maybe Birmingham's going FORWARD has to have its pound of flesh somehow. It's worn patternless in places, at the bar where countless feet have patiently awaited the blunt ministrations of the bar staff, at the door's threshold en route to the toilets. And over in the far corner, the squat bulk of a television projecting out into the room, elbowing its way in to every little grouping, insisting that you cede your discourse to its own. I hate the intrusiveness, its reach into hallowed space. I hate Jerry Springer imposing himself on the room, his contrived antagonism and ratings-chasing cod morality an insult to the real harshness of the lives of the past drinkers. Would the rivet-makers have approved? But of course they, of all people, would have. They'd have loved to have had the Villa piped straight into the bar. And, now, I suppose, it at least provides me with a distraction whilst nursing these triplets.

I'm surrounded by the hum of broad Brummie accent, which is perhaps an unlikely aural comfort blanket, and the always palliative beer. I should be at home in here. But there's an edge on me that I can't put down either to circling solicitors, whose interest anyway waned pretty much the moment our antipathy did, or meetings with women I've long been unable to fathom. Everyone in here seems to be a regular, and has that easy familiarity of nods and grunts that produces community, a protective circumspection that seems exclusionary. Or maybe they're simply wary of winos.

'When you said meet me from work, I didn't think you had this shithole in mind.' Which probably wasn't the most welcoming of welcomes.

'It's convenient isn't it? For you, I mean – it's eight-hundred yards from the station. I didn't want it to entail a special journey so you could sit there with an excuse to play the victim.'

'I didn't realise I played so fragile. Maybe it's your perfume brings out the ethnic in me.'

'I didn't realise you'd gotten so racist. Maybe you've moved on from religion?'

I'm slightly shocked by that outburst, surprised by how tense I suddenly feel, how defensive. Maybe I was sensing glimmers of reconciliatory hope, which might explain though won't have excused the consequent offensive. I take a long, steadying swallow, and she does, too, albeit hers doesn't involve beer. 'You want a drink?' Her demurring doesn't stop me going up again, with the excuse that the queue is down, but we both know we're going to need a little space for this. She sits as I move off, more comfortable in a strange bar than I am, conscious of something more important than to have been found drinking on your own.

When I get back: 'They'll be granting the nisi Tuesday.' She must know that I know this; though I'm still (only just) a divorce virgin, even I can be expected to have grasped where we're at in the court's proceedings. But it is an objective opener. I'm not sure I can trust myself to say anything yet, so I wait for the inevitable subjectivity to develop. 'Once it has started, it's ...' she falters, maybe not having expected to monologue, 'it's ... just going to have a life of its own. You know it'll be unstoppable, if we allow it to get there. You know that.' Do I know that? What I do know these days is that what I thought I knew often turns out to be very much stuff that I didn't know. I didn't, for example, know that it could go quite so tits up quite so quickly. I do know, looking at her now, composed and quietly determined, that I've never stopped fancying her. She always did have a striking freshness about her, an attractiveness that I knew, were it not for the circumstances, would have put her well out of my league. I feel slightly diminished.

We'd been married something like six months before I suggested that we might spice things up a little: maybe it had taken that long for the shock of my good fortune to wear off. Courtesy of her sister, we'd just enjoyed a lock-in at the always less than salubrious Cock Inn, and were risking a weavy walk home. I reckoned on the evening's Diamond White and Stella intake to help lower the tone further. 'D'you fancy dressing up for me one night? Being my little schoolgirl?' Nothing extreme, not the primary school gingham all-in-one, nothing involving nappies for Christ's sake, just the short gym skirt and white socks look, a little white blouse, maybe a school tie slung low below a few undone buttons. St. Clichéians. Which I didn't think an unreasonable request. Not like it's an unusual slip-stream, or anything off the scale. Not for the last time, I'd miscalculated: she flashed me a look, an unspoken interrogation, and then she just turned away. Instantly the very picture of temperate propriety. In the awkward moments that followed, I realised that she was thinking of Georgie, her and now my-by-marriage eight-year-old daughter. Maybe the fact that I'd felt the need for all that Belgian Courage might imply I knew the implications of my asking, knew how the implications would play out for her.

A couple of nights later she was there for me, all dressed up; she'd gone out and bought a navy skirt, some long white socks, even one of the god-awful ginghams – thank God she wasn't wearing it – that even hardened school-reunion aficionados surely must be uncomfortable with. I felt for her, a bit. Asked her, or at least I started to ask, whether she felt ok with it. But she silenced me with a kiss, hard and controlling, which is something she'd never done before. And we never spoke of it again, but I knew, after that first look, that even as she slipped into her role for me, night after night, that there would forever be a tension in her performance, a sick pit-of-stomach feeling over what she might be abetting, what it might precipitate. But even as I felt for her, and I did, those very reservations, that skin-pricking apprehension turned me on as I spread her milky white, white-socked legs. As she coaxes me over decrees nisi, this is one of the things that I do know.

'It wasn't so bad, was it? Was it that bad? We had some good times.' Something else I think I should know, probably without equivocation. How can you do so many years with someone and not have a stash of good times?

'Which good times are we talking about here? The ones where you'd be threatening to storm out at midnight and I'd have to stop you, physically stop you for fear of where you'd end up? The ones where I'd be talking to you via chalk on the bedroom wall because we couldn't actually sit down and speak to one another, couldn't bloody well stand up and shout at each other like normal rowing couples?' I knew I shouldn't have trusted my mouth to speak. 'Other than the sex, we had next to nothing in common. And even that was shot, at the end. And, I seem to remember, the shitness of our shot bedtime routine was one of your recurring complaints.'

'But you never came near me at the end. We were living completely separate lives; you didn't want to sleep with me, you stayed up all hours to avoid any chance of stumbling into a sexual encounter. I felt ... it felt like you didn't fancy me anymore. Do you know how ... let me finish ...' – I'm intent on countering her truth – '... d'you know how unattractive that made me feel?'

'Because you'd just lie there! It was like a Rohypnol practice-run. You wouldn't go down on me. You wouldn't even let *me* go down on *you!*' Which we've obviously touched on before, the actual mechanics of the (in)action that characterized our last couple of semi-celibate years together. It had come up most nights for a while, back then, so there's no novelty in any of this. But it's revision, groundwork, laying a platform for the nub of it all. 'You just had to ask, didn't you? I told you not to, but you had to go and ask them, you had to have them spell it out and lay it down, and of course it was always gonna be "No". Did you tick any other easy stereotypes while you were at it? Ask Mary Whitehouse to a threesome, did you? Fagin for a dime? Clichés tend to give you the answers you go to them for.'

'And this again. You *know* I couldn't, any more, after I knew. How was I supposed to ignore it? How does that work?

But it was just one thing; we could've carried on enjoying a perfectly good sex life without that. It's not everything.'

'But it is and you could, you could. You did, you were, and then, all of a sudden, overnight, you can't. You stop doing something that we both ... *uurrgh* ... because, because some geriatric over in Brooklyn in the good ol' US of A ...' I try to keep it extemporaneous but this has been rehearsed so often, and with such bitterness. ' ... because he no longer fancies the desiccated, three-score years and ten fanny of a missus whose arthritic finger can no longer stroke his walnuted and recalcitrant prostrate, then suddenly going down on your old man is a moral aberration. And from then on, from that point on it's unclean, and every Jehovah's Witness the world over has to stop fucking their husband or their wife in what is by every normal conception of fucking, fucking normal, so that the marital bed may remain clean. Clean ... their catch-all cleanness; how do they define clean, what is this mystic correlation between oral and unclean? Eh? They should be made to announce *that* when they're attempting to seduce you on the doorstep, made to sing it loud and clear: 'We hate to felate / we frown on going down / the Lord has said we can't give head." Probably catchier than any of your Kingdom Melodies, anyway.'

'This is such ... bloody ... hypocrisy. You believed it, remember? You believed as much as I did, that it was true. You were more in the 'Truth' than I was ....'

The charge of believing is true. I'm not so sure that the one of hypocrisy is. When we first met, I believed because I had never known any different; I'd been brought up in it since the age of four, for Jehovah's sake. My world-view was somewhat constrained by anticipation of a 'New World Order', and by the Organisation – 'Mother', we were ... I believe they still are ... encouraged to call it – that prepared you for it. That view inevitably changed when I started secretly peeping beyond the covers of the 'Watchtower' for information about the nature of reality. But either way, it doesn't matter, the accusation really doesn't matter to me a toss (something else they sought to proscribe). 'Can't you see how empty it is? To have your relationship with your God so closely mediated through a third party? The whole point of free will and conscience is that you define yourself through the decisions you make, not have someone else do it all for you. You're not a ... you're not five years old. It's ... they bloody well *demean* it. All the old boys, all those Israelite Patriarchs whom you're supposed to be emulating, they used to row with God about stuff, for God's sake, *with God*, Jonah arguing the toss with God from underneath a gourd tree. Never mind some bloke in a converted office in Brooklyn being beyond questioning. And it's not like he can even get his own prohibitioning straight. I'm all over this now, and Jesus! You wouldn't get your breath. Their record, for an example, on giving head. What a little digging can do ... '

'I'm not really interested in this.'

Which is, of course, the Party Line. She isn't allowed to be interested, really or otherwise, in any of this. Nor will she be allowed to listen to any of it. My sermon will fall upon stony ground because she isn't allowed, in the normal run of things, even to be proximate to one who is critical of 'Mother'.

So, in spite of my diligent researches and the rehearsals they've inspired, she will never learn of the chaotic chronology of JW sexual mores: that, prior to 1974, the bits of your husband and / or wife that you chose to insert into your mouth was a matter only for you and your mouth, and the owner of the bit or bits being so inserted. It was assumed to be nothing to do with the judicial committees and inquisitors that stalked Kingdom Halls to ensure collective conformity. If we'd have settled down, albeit as a five- and a three-year-old, in the early seventies, we could have licked and sucked each other stupid and no-one would have cared. But then the Lord came down on going down, apparently, and communicated to His chosen that it was a big no-no to oral. Unclean, unclean; maybe He'd resurrected that Old Testament thing about not imbibing milk and meat at the same time. A plague on all those who would dare to liven up the penance of monogamy with a little variety. But having so purged, in 1978 He has another change of heart. All those supplications from the frustrated faithful, on knees now bent only in prayer, must have softened His judgement, as did Abraham's entreaties for the Sodomites: 'If I find, oh Lord, just ten righteous men who cannot abide the sentence of missionary intercourse ...' And only then, having let loose a flock of erstwhile frustrated Lovelaces and Reams, and eager lips the Organisation over are everywhere seeking out and docking on their spouses' tumescences, only then does God once more slip into His Whitehouse ways. In 1983, He pronounces that actually He was right in 1974 all along, and that '78 had been just trippy, man, an experience, and now that the cum had cleared, well, your bedroom proclivities are so within His remit after all, and beware any attempt to introduce actual pleasure into your reproductive rutting.

'There's been a decade, a full decade of flip-flopping. Change after change after change. And this is supposed to be the only true religion? The one with the hotline to the Lord? Is He a schizophrenic, your Jehovah?'

'You just better hope, come the Tribulation, that He's an amnesiac. The changes only show how right we are. There's no divine revelation, you know that, there's never been a grand epiphany; it's a light that gradually gets brighter and brighter, and each little unveiling just shows us a bit more of the whole truth. That's what we believe — it's what I believe. It's what *you* believed! It *is* the Truth, and you knew its truth, too, when we first met and you asked me out. How can you not know it now? Look around you, Dave, and see how the prophecies are coming true. How can you not see that it is the Truth?'

I want to expose her truth to her, off-load all that I'd prepared, the stuff that I carry around with me everywhere in case I chance upon a soul to save. 'There's a whole sub-literature of stuff on JWs', I should have been saying. In 1954, Mother had to go to court, and her so-called 'Truth' met with a rival one from the real world. I'd be telling her how their Vice President, Freddie Franz, and the legal beagle Haydon Covington were subpoenaed, and in the course of the trial had to admit that it was all about unity. Unity — *that* was the only Truth to come out of the exchange: 'Unity at all costs', he conceded, under oath, 'unity at all costs, even if it's based upon enforced acceptance of false prophecy'. Actually in the transcript – I memorized it when I found it, the 'enforced acceptance of false prophecy'. Everyone has to sing from the same bull-sheet.

I'm looking over at her as all this goes through my head, but manage to stop it before my tongue gets a hold of it. There was no need to be so sharp with her, and I'm moved now, guilty over the distress that my attempts to shake her into waking have caused, pain that is writ large in her eyes. If only she could step out of it for just a moment, experience just one moment of clarity, and examine the Foucauldian conceit, the self-affirming Orwellian act of calling it 'The Truth' in the first place. The continuous subconscious reaffirmation in the act of repeating it, so that 'the Word becomes flesh'. But of course, I can't but sympathize even as I trash it – which is maybe why I allowed it to get nasty. I've been there, defending the indefensible against the reproaches of evidence and logic, supported by the mantric chants of all those Kingdom Melodies. 'God has brought us into his fold. / We enjoy the things he foretold. / Unity and peace we possess, / bringing such happiness.' Dozens of times a year, before a chastening Watchtower study or a sanctimonious sermon about the dangers of 'independent thinking'. 'Unity we cherish; / harmony is sweet.' Oh, there's quite a repertoire, a whole catalogue of subliminal on-messaging: 'In God's work there's much to be done. / He directs us now through his son. / May we serve obediently, / working in harmony. / As we pray for oneness of mind, / and we all take care to be kind ...'

I've moved on from upsetting her soul with my attempts to save it, and am remembering now the Robert Frank picture that hangs on my wall, of an old guy back in 1950s New York, booted and suited but with a mien of lugubrious resignation, a copy of the Watchtower in his thrust-forward hand. I bought it as a chastener to my own thrusting time, to how prophesies and deadlines pass and die and yet somehow their adherents still hang on in there. It's there, hung on the wall in my front room, a talisman against the sophistry of the numinescent, the seductiveness of millenarianism. But when she saw it, she lit up and connected with him, our Old Joe, and saw in him a lineage and a history, a reach back to the past that merely validated the present. 'These all died in faith, not having received the promises, but having seen them afar off.' Solidarity, the perseverance of the brotherhood, the faith of the faithful of old. Nothing of the delusion, the error, the change, the waste. One impassive old face staring out, and yet how different our reactions to it. 'Unity and peace we possess, / bringing such happiness.' 'The 'Truth'?' I content myself with a desultory retort: 'It should be called The Imposition, more like'.

She's telling me that she didn't come here to talk about the Witnesses, but about us, and I'm anyway tuning out from them now, and on to our unity, in the early days, in the first post-wedding flush, all that good, adventurous – for a while school-girl – sex, before the interpolation of those thrusting Watchtowers.

'Dave, I came here to see if we could avoid next week somehow. Isn't there something worth saving?'

'I'm sorry. No, really I am, sorrier than you think, than probably is coming across. But we tried it with Mother in the bed, with Her as our constant bedtime companion, a Witness á trois, and I don't see how it would work out any better now. Not for me, not for you. I'm bitter about the whole JW thing, not just blowjobs. For God's sake, blowjobs?'

'I need to move on, and I need to know whether you're coming with me.' Whether I do come or I don't, she won't be travelling alone. Something else I'm pretty sure I know. And paradoxically, I'm glad, sort of, that she'll be taking Him along. He gets her through, with that placebo of belief. Jehovah. And His flock, too, even though I see them as a cowed crutch of the obedient, an international brotherhood of the subdued. Which is probably unfair, I think I know. Even in the maelstrom of our implosion, I remember how she would set out for her meetings, Sunday and Tuesday and Thursday, resolute despite the weather and my antipathy, to the warm place that was her Hall. She relied on it and was succoured by it, when there was so little else for her. The hope and the help of the Father. And having once had it myself and having now lost it, I envy her, I envy all of them that. I miss Him. It was always Mother who exorcised me, a Mother unfit for the role She arrogates to herself, authoritarian and spiteful, wilful, nasty, and vindictive. Is that what She thinks the Old Man stands for? Maybe it's a corporate case of Munchausen's Syndrome by Proxy, a psychological malfunction inflicted on an international, organisational scale. Which, I always thought, was something of a misreading of Him.

But now there are tears. And what is it with random blokes in random pubs, feeling that they can be provoked by the unsolicited tears of soon-to-be ex-wives?

5

'Hi, it's Jenna, can you book me sick?' This was from the Bear's car park. Earlier in the morning, first thing in front of the mirror, I'd gotten myself a salute by the briefly yellow ring that I knew would soon be intent on blacking up, giving me the full-on minstrel treatment. Soon I'd be walking round with a big, bold question mark all over my face, which would mean me having to offer up repeated explanations all week. And it wasn't to be helped this morning by the Stella-induced blood-shot eyes that are the bequest of late night self-pity. Not a good look. But I'd intended to go in, nevertheless, had there and then resigned myself to a day's piss-taking interrogation, if only to get it out of the way. Which may, I don't know, may perhaps have just been bloody-mindedness over the Lord's travelling arrangements. But I packed my stuff, drove down, parked up. There'd be no chance of Damascene bounce this morning, I knew that much from the off, and sure enough, as I opened the door and stepped out onto the car park, there was the Bristol Road stretching itself out into something like a trial. It shuddered, as I leaned on the car's roof, it shuddered in the hangover.

    Bounce or no, I suppose I'd hoped for routine to take over. Stood leant by the open car door, bag in hand, I was waiting for the feet to move off, waiting for my unoccupied hand to reach out and slam the door, to remote lock it. But there was nothing. There was nothing on auto. And then Old Joe moved and began beating out eight o'clock, as is *his* routine, but this time, and I don't know why, this time he reminded me of Stef. I thought of Stef – my Effie – about whom I haven't had a passing thought for I don't know how long; she chooses today, of all my preoccupied days, to push back into my conscious. And I knew then that I really couldn't be bothered, after all. It was time to get back into the car and use up some sick leave.

Use up some of my allocation. Though it'd have to be with something anodyne, something that wouldn't leave them with threads over which to go speculating. Telling them that I'd 'got smacked, and won't be in 'til the eye goes down' wasn't an especially attractive option. Diarrhoea, of course, is the easy default, the one that everyone reaches for because they think people actually worry about spelling it correctly on a PR12. But she'd annoyed me; for what was the first time, really, I had been wound up by Stephanie, and so I just called in with stress.

I had expected her to be around from the off, twelve, eighteen months ago, when I first started parking up here as part of my revenge on Bertie. I'd expected her to be there waiting, a ghostly presence inhabiting the car park in which, like Salome, she'd sucked me in with her merry dance, albeit one of which she herself was unaware. A *Siren Insciens*. So, initially, I'd balked at using it, because I couldn't be doing with the unsettling aftertaste that I presumed she'd be trailing. But despite all the trepidation, I found there was nothing, no hint of her when I'd be walking surreptitiously past the locked and shuttered bar doors, no ache, no pit of stomach stuff, maybe just a detached acknowledgement of a shared hinterland, a cursory nod to a past. For a year and more it seems I'd been happy to have her slipped into mere acquaintance, been happy to forget her pretty well the moment I got out of the car and onto the Bristol Road. And it had shocked me, when after a few mornings it had seemed a *fait accompli*, that it was mission accomplished: I'd always thought that she was and would ever be under my skin. Maybe cerebral connexions don't last after all, maybe cum is the better coagulant. Effie. Stephanie Vine, the most unlikely of barmaids. And now, of all days, I find her pushing her way back into my life.

I met her at University, not in the bar. She was what you might call mousy, habituated to the backs of rooms, the ends of rows, and as I was often late to lectures we ended up sharing space. She was a reluctant sharer, though; for weeks, she'd sit skulking behind skinny, hunkered-forward shoulders that were like two gaunt chaperones, always one between us whichever side I happened to be sat, starchy and prim, trying to partition and control space. Only when she realised that I was likely to be a recurring feature of her lecture hall legroom did she begin even to acknowledge me, at first just the slightest nod of a greeting, and sometimes a small exhalation to accompany a flash of eye contact. I'd smile back, of course, and hello. But the most I got was a fleeting if sweet upturn of the mouth.

I suppose I must have spent quite a while peering at her, over the weeks. Not intentionally aggressively, not in any way as a provocation, merely as a curious observer. She rarely reciprocated the interest, or certainly she didn't give any indication of it. Just quietly seethed, probably, at the intrusive nob at the end of the row. No wonder she stayed hunched up in a parody of studious, concentrated note-taking. She was model thin, with a grace that she tried to overcome with a combination of that contorted posture and a series of baggy, shapeless jumpers and a Parker. Lazily, I took it all as shorthand for standard student activism, down with all figurations of physical beauty and its consequent objectification of women, that sort of stuff. Though I couldn't see her having any bras to burn. For weeks, she was an impenetrable bundle of defensiveness, a reserve that I could so easily have taken for a savage aloofness. But there was something behind those however brief smiling interludes, an indication of her being distant in spite of herself, of a desire to come out to play. So I watched as discreetly as I could, not wanting to risk spooking her or have her just disappear out of lectures. She was too intriguing. I wanted to be around when that mouse found its roar. It translated out into the most coquettish of miens, all puppyish eyes, a sort of submissive feint. I found it a mesmeric confection. I so wanted to fuck her. But I seemed to be no more than a presence in her peripheral space.

It was a conference that brought us together. A tranche of feminism, of all things, that most unlikely of heterosexual match-makers; an entire day on how the love of penis is the root of all evil, that sort of stuff. Not usually my bag, but I'd been intrigued by the title of one of the papers: 'Between

Faeces and Urine: the Architectural Coherence of Female Genitalia'. I heard in it an echo of one of Paglia's disquisitions, one of those in which she celebrates male projection, where 'male urination really is a kind of accomplishment, an arc of transcendence.' After reading it, I would never again take my transcending piss for granted. And from then on I've had something of a hard spot for Camille, for the manner in which she butchers sacred heifers. Ballsy, provocative and, unusually for an academic, eminently readable. But I suppose it was inevitable, given the remit of these conferences, that Paglia was in for a traducing. No way were they going to tolerate that sort of entrenchment on the gender front. I reckon I managed about twenty minutes of the stultifying rant on genital design and its metaphysical symbolism, but then something just irrupted, and a non-too-whispered 'bollocks' tumbled out in support of her. Which, given her defence of it, I thought an appropriate deployment of the male apparatus, to cheerlead for her in absentia. And then, from just down the row, just as heads of opprobrium were turning my way, 'and occasionally cunts, too'. Ah, so maybe it really was a lazy shorthand; maybe Effie is a fellow cheerer after all, albeit one with a slightly quieter pom-pom. Her head was popped out and round her shoulder, with just a trace of that grin: I suddenly felt like Doctor Doolittle, able to talk turtle. It was the loudest – no, the only – real noise I'd ever heard come out of her, all half dozen or so syllables of it in a delightful, completely incongruent twang of Newcastle Braun. Of itself, it amounted to nothing over-familiar, of course, nothing that could be mistaken for an invitation to spend the night. Under the now divided glare of disapproving fellow delegates, she was straight away back in to her hunch, and furiously scribbling down her notes again. But I recognise a tentative reach-out when I'm handed one.

'All that hostility, and there was I thinking that discussing genitals was the whole point of the conference.' This in an altogether quieter whisper. She'd shifted all her stuff across to accommodate me as soon as the paper had ended, and I'd moved in to take her up on the non-too conventional how-do-you-do.

'And there was me thinking that you were a card-carrying misandrist.'

'Maybe I am. What I said could be construed in any number of ways. Perhaps I was being ironic.'

'I think the general consensus went with me. Unless it's that none of them can bear to hear the vulva word spoken aloud. Too sacred.'

A week ago I couldn't even get an hello out of her, and now here we sit freely discussing the sisterhood's reproductive organs. Even though she's now turned down to a murmur so as not to provoke the devoted, and her hands pull constantly at her sleeves in a way that's suggestive of some sort of compulsion, I still have difficulty reconciling this performance with mouse-girl.

'Tread carefully around sacred spaces. They sometimes bite.'

'Noted. For future careful treading.' I hoped that that wasn't too forward; she seemed to be drifting off again, back to her own note-taking, but she'd anyway seemed quite focused on this next paper since its being introduced. 'The Master's Eye: Early Mediaeval Pedagogic Practice.' I decided to just go back to watching her.

*

Five o'clock. The last paper of any conference is often tricky; they seem designed to leave a trail of premises hanging, on to which the chair (woman, in this case) can attach invitations to little cheese and cracker hustings or extra plenary sessions, and into which the eager are invariably sucked. And I'm conscious of the eager note-taking that's been going on beside me for the last three or four hours, give or take the odd 'cunt'. I'm desperate not to lose what little momentum I seem to have recently accrued to a cheesy nibbles get-together, in which I can imagine her reverting to that sullen, defensive default. I've got the maybe ten seconds of applause to come up with something.

'You going to the plenary?' So, all things considered, a pretty piss-poor opener. 'Paglia's nemesis is holding court. We could continue the baiting.'

'No, I don't reckon I can be bothered, thanks anyway. I think I've done my feminist penance for today.' So is that the knock back I think it might be? I imagine myself as the sort of flagellation she sees herself as having to endure whenever she turns up to seminars, lectures, student-whatevers, the flailing tail of which she cannot wait to be done with. That verbal playfulness merely a means to pass it the quicker; engaging with the lash. She's slightly crumpled again, slightly hunched in an echo of her lecture-hall posture. I don't know whether to feel protective or annoyed. Briefly she looks up, over that shoulder: 'Fancy a quick one somewhere, off campus if you like?' She's looking for feedback. 'The Bear is just up the road – I've got to be there in an hour anyway.' And, in response to my raised eyebrows, 'I do the evenings, some of them, and over the weekend.' That she was bar staff was even more shocking than my being able to talk to the animals. Bar workers are defined by their insouciance, surely, their self-possessedness. I just couldn't see that sort of softness operating on the wrong side of the counter.

Of course I went, and of course I would wait for her to finish her shift. We'd had just time enough for her to down a lemon and lime while I started on the first of a few Bathams, and then I played with a crossword while she pared down her overdraft. At about ten-forty I finished off and folded up, waited for probably ten minutes to catch sight of her, and having given up went out to sit in the motor. The car park was bleak, badly lit, and what little moon there was had to filter through that bank of skinny poplars over on the far side, leaving indistinct lines of shadow striping the tarmac. And then at about twenty-past the three of them appeared in the doorway, Stef and her entourage. She stopped briefly before coming out, just to check to see that I actually had stayed, as though she'd no right to expect me to have been there; I imagine it always will be the triumph of expectation over hope, with Stef. And then, having seen me, she bowled over with her head down, hands thrust into her pockets, just another sullen teenager scuttling across the tarmac.

'I didn't expect you to wait. You needn't have, I usually walk it.'

'Oh I had to. If only to convince myself that this isn't some elaborate ruse, part of a Jeremy Beadle set-up. That you do actually work in a bar.'

'And how did I do? How was my Bathams? Not too much top?'

'No, excellent, no. A perfect head; you do give good head.'

'I also give good weed. If that's not going to burst too many of your preconceptions.'

'Didn't realise you were so far off the rails. Are you going to really rattle me, and do a one-handed roll?'

'No, I'm not that bad, not yet. Though I'm working on it. I reckon I just need to get with a dodgier circle of friends.'

Dodgier circle? I'm trying not to let the Bathams let me snort, and trying to keep my not snorting from her while thinking that any circle would be a start. But she's learned an impressive rolling technique from somewhere; her thin fingers slip into and around her smoking pouch with an easy familiarity, and produce a tight, lean clip in no time. She draws deep on it, to get it fired up, and then hands it over with a murmured 'Pot, kettle, black.'

'I know, I know. I just struggle with the others' – I take a deep pull of my own – 'they seem to be a wholly different species. And I get to where I just cannot be bothered.'

She takes it back: 'Oh I'm bothered. I cannot just be.'

*

Bathams and skunk conspire to produce the most delicious of woozinesses. I drop down the window and a cool blast of early morning wheels in, bringing along with it the smell that damp starts have and that I think I'm going to be walking home with. I know from past experience not to inhale too quickly, too eagerly, but she's brought some good stuff along, with a mellow follow on that cups you in love.

'I appreciate it's probably a bit early for me to be going in to a jealous boyfriend routine, but who was the guy at the bar? Tall chap, offensively good looking. Just that you seemed very relaxed with him. Almost' – another puff – 'as relaxed as you are now.'

'Because relaxed and chatty isn't what I do, right? Stands out that much?'

'No, only that ...'

'He's my brother. He's up from London for a couple of days, maybe a while longer. Taking an Art College sabbatical while he ponders his next brush stroke. And yes, we've pretty much managed to avoid the sibling rivalry thing.'

'Probably a shame that you have. For him. Better for his Muse if there'd been screaming and antagonism and unresolved sexual tension.' The freshness of the air is starting to toy with me. 'Joking. Close is always good. I'm sure you were the very definition of fairness in sharing your Smarties. Regular happy families, with lots of rabbits and hamsters. And long walks Sunday afternoons, everybody hand in hand.'

'Don't you love this bit? The feeling of freedom and weightlessness and peace. It leaves me so I don't care anymore, about anything.'

'So why not skunk out more often? Hook up, take it intravenously.'

'So you can hit some more student stereotypes?' She cracks open her own window; 'For some reason, I seem to have decided that you're safe enough to wind down with. We don't seem so different.' Ah, so it's the kindred of the peripheried, is it? We fellow travellers. I wonder whether it's too much to hope it might someday become a we fellow fucked?

'As I've said, I got to where I couldn't be bothered. And I have the excuse that I was abused; I've had the Lord down my pants since I don't know when.' I wonder if my eyes are as dilated as hers, two wonderfully deep moons drifting off into contentment.

'I just didn't start well. Fell out with one of the girls in the block in the first year and she made my life hell, and I never really picked it up after that. She used to kick my stuff, all my personal stuff, you know ... She kicked everything round the kitchen and off the balcony. And when you disconnect at the beginning, it just becomes so difficult to make it up. With any of them. It's like a physical thing, like the synapse that connects you and them has been damaged, and so it becomes impossible to relax and ingratiate.' I am realising that the drifting wasn't into peace but into melancholy, and that there might be tears somewhere close by. She suddenly blows smoke into my face, I assume as a diversion, but even so it's an intimacy that I couldn't have conceived of just a couple of hours ago. I find myself hardening. I can smell her, even through the evening's work and the weed and the morning's damp; she smells of aloe, of having just washed, of meticulous, maybe compulsive cleanness. I hope all of these confessions and neuroses won't prevent me from someday strapping her to the posts of my bed.

'What goes around ...' and immediately I hate myself for it, for throwing easy platitudes at her. She draws again on the joint, deep. 'Is that where the disparity comes from? Between the you out here and the you in the lecture hall? Because we haven't had chance to damage our synapse?' She passes the roll across and just exhales in to my face again, looking hard at me. I can't read where she's at, and so decide to move on to safer ground. 'He's a good-looking bastard, I have to say. I hate him already, him and his gene pool. Your indecisive brother.'

'They fuck you up.'

'Mmm'. I'm finishing my pull, glad that the awkwardness has passed. 'I know the poem. Unless, of course, we've suddenly gone back to talking about feminists ...'

'I was fourteen.' She pauses, as though deciding whether or not to step off. 'And he came in, and just ...'

'Whoa, hang on there. Are you sure that what I think you're about to do is really what you want to be doing? I mean, I'm happy, I'm more than happy to be a shoulder, but in the cold ...'

'I knew, I knew. Of course I knew. I'd heard the rows, I knew what was going on. He knocked, uncertainly, all hesitant, and then came in anyway, just came in and sat at the head of the bed. With his back to the wall. Which was their wall, too. Didn't say a word, just sat there and ran his fingers through my hair the way he used to, years before, when I was a kid. And then he started, he just started banging his head backwards, banging and banging and banging for ages. I remember the slow rhythm of it on the bedroom wall. Smacking his head on the wall, pleading with her to stop sleeping with his mate.'

I don't know how many times and to how many people she's revealed that, but I reckon not many because it has smashed her. As the words tripped out I watched her folding in on herself, crumpling in front of both the fact and the sharing of it. What was I supposed to do? I had nothing for her but an arm and a squeeze, that belated shoulder, and empathy for a fourteen-year-old lying bewildered and quivering in a bed somewhere up north sometime in the past. I started to stroke her head, my fingers reaching out into her scalp, into her pain, and then I had to hope that they weren't for her a sickening parody of his fingers, his stroking, four, five, however many years ago.

What is it with sex? What, exactly, is it? As I gently distanced my fingers she came up from her crouch, every word of that confiding having depleted her, and shook off my awkward arm and took my head in her hands. And then her tongue was pushing into my mouth, needy and urgent, questing, and then her left hand was wandering down, pressing against my still swollen cock – even as I'm desperate for it not to be swollen – pressing against it, stroking it, grabbing it, almost pushing it back, as though she were trying to save me from something, maybe, something like a hernia.

'Whoa.' Again. Though I'd later wonder about this one. 'Are you sure this is quite what you need just now, at this moment?'

Old Joe chimes two through the open windows, and what with the early morning moon and the bells and my woozy weltanshauung, it should have been quite a romantic moment.

She lets me stroke the top of her knee, a single, outstretched index finger transcribing an endless figure of eight; it traces out the twin circles, one of them chasing round the patella, the other moving off in a looping elliptical orbit over the smooth mound of her vastus medialis oblique. Her knees part almost imperceptibly as the finger slowly works its meandering way down to the tendons behind the joint. It's supposed to be soothing, and ameliorating, and is known to strengthen synapses. I didn't know then that I'd never see her again.

*

Our ad hoc arrangement, made early on in a conference that I couldn't take seriously after our impromptu contribution to it, had been to meet up the following morning, ostensibly to go over such notes as we had. Given that some of it had touched unexpectedly on a pending essay topic, I was hoping to avail myself of all of Stef's studiousness – and maybe, after that night in the car park, of her generosity, period. Ten or thereabouts, in the Mason Lounge. We'd kept the time intentionally vague; I'm not normally the most punctual of people, though I'd be astonished if that were true of her. But today, I was there for ten, and took up a couch on the far side of the room, opposite the double doors, tucked away from the thoroughfare. In the hope, I suppose. When eleven came by and she still hadn't, I allowed myself to be surprised and maybe a little annoyed. I gave it until twelve, but there are only so many times you can sift through notes and then reading lists and assignments for the following week, under the pretence that she might just be running a little late.

When, at the next lecture, the back row was devoid of skulking teenagers, I tracked down a number for her. It rang through its default cycle of rings before the answerphone cut in. Her disembodied northern voice sounded as incongruous as it had the first time I'd heard it, suffused with that same playfulness with which she'd allowed me to become familiar. 'Hi, it's Stef, obviously. Make it sufficiently interesting for me to wanna get back to you.' Where the fuck is the all-confessing, psyche-stripping, cock-squashing girl who let me in last night? Is that interesting enough for you? Over the afternoon, I twice tried to leave something, anything that might overcome that starting pistol of a bleep to just put us back into the easy-going, relaxed, Bear-car park mind-set. But nothing came that wouldn't have sounded forced and desperate. And then she evidently got tired of listening in to non-messages, to being silenced at, because on my third attempt at ringing she answered with a weak, wary 'Hello?' I suppose she must have anticipated that I'd be ringing sometime.

I didn't ask about the Mason non-show. Why would I, first off? But I reckoned on the lecture being safe ground – it was something that remained firmly in the public, in the expected space.

'I'm not doing it anymore. I've knocked it on the head.' And with those few words she announced her retreat to Newcastle, to not academia, to not me. Not that it had anything to do with me, or with last night: 'Don't flatter yourself', which isn't her in either of her guises; the tartness seemed a convenient way of foreclosing the subject. No, it'd been brewing for a time, and her uncharacteristically tactile advance was merely coincidental. She'd already informed the Student Office.

I would wonder for a while afterwards whether it had had anything to do with the configuration of my genitals, whether she'd thought their architecture to be incoherent, or something. Which is in no way an elegant variation on the 'she doesn't fancy me, she must therefore be gay' self-preserving deceit. I'd had sufficient experience of rejection on its own merits, and indeed have sufficient dignity, not to be in need of that sort of ruse. But when some space had opened up, a little distance between it and my thinking about it, then the forcedness, the impromptu desperate energy of that kiss came to seem experimental, somehow. As if she were trying finally to sort something out, to prove something to herself. In retrospect, I wished that she had offered it up as an excuse or a rationale. It would have given me something to counter, however half-heartedly. 'You're into the clitoris? Then I'm your man. Surely you discovered that, if nothing else, from the peremptory grope that night. Maybe I didn't tell you that as her parting shot my then newly-ex-girlfriend told me she was tired of the lesbian experimentation. This really isn't a phallus to fear.'

But of course it wasn't the phallus that she feared, it was the proximity. The proximity to intimacy. And not even, or not just, sexual intimacy. The whole opening up and laying herself bare and lying next to someone as they got similarly naked. Me, the other students, the necessity of arguing a position, and what it might reveal, that is a requirement for graduation and certainly for study beyond. I obviously didn't enquire, I would never have enquired about her sexual proclivities; I started to rail at her instead for not mentioning any of it, for keeping it all to herself, for what I perceived to be her betrayal of me when we'd gone so far down the confessional route: 'You let me in on all that about your dad, about your parents, for Christ's sake,' type of stuff. I thought we'd connected, and certainly I'd hooked on to her, on to her dry wit and her point of view. But, it seemed, Effie was with the ex. She just wanted to wave goodbye. Towards what would become the end of the conversation, when she perhaps realised that I was leaning – for her, a little too heavily – on her rejection of my friendship rather than of my cock, I got a glimpse of the rage on which all that well-practised deference was sitting. A hint of roar. She knew how much I liked her, how much I wanted to be around her, and she'd maybe foreseen herself leaning on the wanting. Seems I was a crutch she didn't trust herself to be touching.

What's strange is that she's suddenly in my thoughts, when I've been using the car park for more than a year now without so much as a peep out of her. And I'm not sure what it means for me to be revisiting with such fondness such a doomed double act.

6

So she isn't happy in her work. Many of us aren't: I reckon just about everyone working here will, at some stage, have had to drag an unwilling self into an unwelcoming dawn. But much of what our job entails is sufficiently distanced from any end product for us to remain indifferent to our indifference. The consequences of an apathetic approach to testing fire-ground pumps or to polishing small axes don't manifest themselves the moment we forge a record or put back a still-rusty hatchet. We hide behind the casuistry that we'll likely never have to deal with the effects of our neglect first-hand. And anyway, our omissions are not necessarily a case of our not wanting to be here, but rather small acts of rebellion. So we aren't diminished by them.

Rita's disinterest is more self-assured. She seems happy to confront its effects face-to-face and daily, to the point where a few of us think she might now even be contriving the interface. Which must present her with something of a dilemma: there is no doubt that she cannot stand to be here, attending to the most elemental needs of our flesh, and yet I've never known her miss a day, never even known her be late, seemingly that she may demonstrate to us the intensity of her disdain. Perhaps the dynamic of the paradox is distracting in a way that cooking would appear not to be.

She rolled it out with our toast break, must be a couple of years after starting here. At ten-twenty-five on the dot, we'd find her busying herself at the toaster, lining them up for our eleven o'clock down time. Hunching over the moment we walked in, her shoulders winged as though she were a hawk shielding a kill. As each barely browned slice popped up, she'd have it out and swiped with margarine, and then away into the hotplate, piling each one on top of the other. And then the still warm, still gently steaming rounds would rest there for thirty-five minutes, like a piece of topside, so that when we got to them they were brittle and crisp on the outside, moist in the middle. They would ripple and corrugate, orogenesis in miniature, tearing as we attempted marmite.

But her toast was just an hors d'oeuvre. She's been working on her mains; pork chops, last week, that she deigned to hot griddle for us, and a farmers' market cauliflower that she somehow thought to steam, with a pinch of salt even, all of it served with some of the potatoes that we'd had left over from the previous week. Cooked as she'd been handed them –last season's spuds that had lain for a week on top of a warm mess cupboard – perfectly boiled in a little salted water but otherwise untouched, served as they were, the half-inch-long white chits reaching out through her thick gravy like anaemic little Atlantian hands. Maybe she'd thought of them as one of our five a day, an exotic variation on bean sprouts or something. If she thought of them at all. And so indifferent, as she'd handed each of us a plate, to the point of churlishness.

Of course it was all softly, softly at first, don't fuck with the hand that feeds you, diplomacy to a degree that I think would probably be shocking to us now. An unusual and quiet sobriety would descend on the mess room as with grim resignation we'd try to force down dinner after fucked over dinner, so that we might hand her back something like a half-cleared plate. Conscientiously we avoided the confrontation she sought to provoke. But inevitably it gave out, and quite some time before she started putting Triffid on the menu; for six, eight months now, the watches have been about as inclined to disguise their contempt as she has her asperity, which, other than salt, seems to be one of the few seasonings she stretches to. Plates of untouched food pass between kitchen and mess table as though, ironically enough, they're on one of those conveyors that move half decent sushi around some high class place. So, logically enough, we conclude that she doesn't love her work. Or is it just that we don't appreciate the way she loves it? Maybe her anti-performance really is nothing more or less than an acute version of our own neglect: she turns in, day after day, her quest to ensure that the appetites that she feels have not deserved satisfaction, do not get satisfied. Our unsolid days undeserving of her solid meals: 'If any would not work, neither let him eat,' sort of stuff. Or at least eat with any pleasure; maybe we are her project.

In my newish role as mess-man, I've taken it upon myself not to capitulate in all of this, not to roll over and have her force us all down the sandwich route so she can do Jack Shit for four hours, polishing her Sudoku prowess. There is a weight of responsibility here that's curiously absent from all the testing and the cleaning – an 'ownership' of the issue, if we were to stoop to Fire Brigade parlance. Having got some of the boys on message, I've decided to try playing good cop to Jim Kelly's bad. Ned had a spat with her over his elevenses: it seems you can't make an omelette without breaking egg shells into it. The eventual row was explosive, public and then tearful, and for about two weeks Bad Cop appeared to have won out. But then the shells reappeared with a vengeance, and Ned resigned himself to cooking his own omelettes whilst the cook, her arms folded, looked on. I'm trying to coax her into jerking some chicken.

'It's all done for you. I'll get a packet that you just sprinkle over the chicken and then leave. Ready-made marinade, stick it in the oven, boil up some rice.'

The bait remained untaken. She was stood with her back to me over at one of the sinks, in what I assumed to be a defensive posture; all four taps were turned fully on, the water thundering down into the two bowls to produce a thick, frothy lather that I was sure she hoped she wouldn't have any use for.

'It's going to be easier than knocking up all the veg for a chicken dinner ...'

Still not much of a bite. As she moved between the sinks, whisking the water meaninglessly, the hem of her white coat sashayed to and fro against the back of her bare legs, bouncing off and tapping against the drop of her thighs at the point where they pull in to the knee. They are clammy, and pale, and pocked with a smattering of freckles. I suddenly realised just how short it must be, whatever it is that she is wearing beneath it. And then found myself imagining her maybe pulling it up, when she gets home, or when he gets in from wherever, and those puddingy thighs spreading to embrace the considerable bulk that is her corpulent husband's waist and groin, cupping around him and pulling him in and on. Her ankles two hooks in him.

'And the boys will be good for it, they love anything a little bit out of the ordinary.' Her contrapuntal moaning setting off his panting grunts. Or maybe she just lies back, and thinks of cupcakes. 'Hidy will adore you for it. In fact it was him who suggested it.' She's intrigued with Hide, his poisonous caprice – maybe sees him as a potential ally, after the incident with Ned.

'So, was he a big bloke,' she countered, without so much as a look over her shoulder, 'or were you just pissed?'

I wasn't going to let that faze me, to let it cause any mission creep; I'd already had two hours of it since the beginning of the shift. Yeah, yeah, was I a-talking when I should've been a-listening? Did you make a mess of his hands? Yadda yadda, blah, blah...

I didn't join to be a mess-man, didn't go through fourteen ball-breaking weeks of initial training to spend my mornings bouncing around the local pensioners, competing over specials on chicken breasts so that I could balance a budget and soft-soap a cook into cooking. I wanted to be on a truck, even more – this was at the beginning, remember – even more than I wanted to be on leave. Something to do with the adrenaline rushes, yes, but it wasn't just about the rush in the moment; decent jobs were a currency, traded around the bar for weeks after the event. In the early days, when it used to matter, having been at a certain job and thereby having something to contribute to the constant, almost obsessive recycled reliving of it allowed you in. For the duration of the discussion, at least, you were fully a part of the group. Framed like that it makes you think of OJ, and his mess tables.

One of my first jobs, with Benny, was a sprawling Victorian three-storey, well alight, starting to vent out of one of the upstairs windows. When we tip up to it, there's a guy screaming that somebody's still in there. 'Bread and butter stuff', was all I could hear as I started up, the training school mantra of Barry Perry kicking in in my ear. We groped our way in below the heat layer, hands and knees, blind as a couple of moles. No more than three feet behind him, and I was having to track him by the asthmatic rasp of his demand valve, his laboured inhaling and exhaling amplified through the filters and pulleys of his mask. Our torches not even beginning to push at the blackness. At the top of the stairs, he turned right into a room and bawled at me to check left. I fumbled around, groping for a hallway or doorway, anything recognisable, traced the skirting until it stopped and opened out. And all the time the anticipation, the sickening ambivalent wanting and not wanting to bump into the tell-tale dead weight of unconscious flesh.

Somewhere, there's a fire still pumping. My ears haven't felt that perversely reassuring searing bitch-slap of steam, so I know no-one's hit it yet. Inching forward; every shuffle-space has to be pawed over, checked physically with outstretched fingers groping for anything identifiable. I can feel the insides of my gloves beginning to scald, and try to avoid my hands touching the hot leather, but how do you manage that when you're on all fours? Adrenaline is devouring my air. I have no idea where this ends. 'Benny. *Benny.*' Already the heat, the void, is goading my buttons. I can't even find the bed in here. Where's the fucking bed? But then I can hear his demand-valve-wheezing again, somewhere, about seven or eight feet away. 'Benny'. And then he's here, next to me at last, shouting into where he thinks my ear might be, between his own gasping intakes of breath, trying to synchronize the out and the in, shouting something about the top floor.

Never lose contact. That's 'day-one, lesson-one stuff': another pithy Perryism. Always stay within physical contact of your partner, because in there, when everything else, every one of your senses, is being fucked with, that insistent, reaffirming touch of your partner is the only thing you've got. The only thing connecting you with an outside. A couple of blind men edging along a slide-rule of fear and pain, not sure where the end is or the edges are; having to negotiate with a recalcitrant rubber diaphragm for every breath; facing down the urge to shy away from the repeated smack of the heat. How far are you willing to go with this? Where, exactly, is your limit? So you stay with your buddy; he's like your comfort rag, your S & M safe word.

We brought that Edward Road house fire into the bar for weeks after, relived the heat, compared blisters, went over the approach and the tactics. Wondered if we could have saved the stiff, somehow. I felt for a while that I'd been allowed to come close to him, to Benny, my partner for the night; a real connexion forged through a traumatic shared experience. But for years now it's a buzz that has existed only as a memory, like a feeling that someone else has had and is trying to communicate to me, a vicarious, projected experience. There's a decade and a half of disillusionment between us.

My concern this morning is with where my illusionment seems to be coming from now. What is it with suddenly needing to have her cook for us? Why am I so preoccupied with a day's work for a day's pay? Given my general indifference to all things fire brigade, her machinations at the cooker should have been a welcome excuse. Why had *I* not been embraced, albeit as an indolent rather than an insidious ally; why not let sleeping cooks lie? For a couple of weeks or more, my energies have been directed towards and satisfied by the most mundane and middle-aged of concerns. And for I don't know how many years they've been divorced from what I once considered to be such an intrinsic part of me. What's most troubling is that I can't even begin to put my finger on the shift.

*

It has managed to retain a certain grandeur about itself, echoes of Victorian gravitas that it's dragged over from a corseted and bonneted yesteryear. Big, imperious bricks squeezing the mortar into thin seams, which when you're stood from a way back offers up the frontage as a sweeping solid block of terracotta. Large bay windows on either side of the doorway rise up through its three storys, the roofs of both columns capped by a run of slightly ostentatious fleur-de-lys ridge tiles, and elegant swan neck finials that make me think of a choreographed double suicide in mid lunge. But then you catch sight of the banks of letterboxes and bells that rash the front entrance, and it loses a little of the impact; difficult, I suppose, for a house that's had its insides carved up into single accommodations to project much hauteur on the outside. After all these years, I doubt any of the residents in there would know anything of our shared history.

It looks out over Calthorpe Park, which even now offers up a pretty fine view for what is in reality the interstice between albeit past splendour and failed sixties social intervention. From this side, the side of past glories, the bandstand takes centre stage, an ornate cast iron hexagonal in City of Birmingham red and blue that I imagine must be quite striking against the summer flush of its flower borders. Over the top, beyond the high screen of holly and ash and sycamore, a cityscape of modest skyscrapers and multi-storey car parks. He'd have had a good view through that wide expanse of his second floor bay window, might even have been able to make out the top of the onion of the Central Mosque, over the crowns of the trees. If he'd been minded to. I'd have spent time sat at that window, had it been my window, especially in the summer when of all this explodes into colour, sweeping flower-beds and freshly painted park furniture. I take off my hat to them, the Council's Parks and Gardens. Although maybe it's all just a desperate mea culpa to the residents round here, money for a grand floral apology being easier to find than a resolution to the druggies and working girls that haunt it. Now that we're speeding headlong into winter, it's all a little drab and tired, etiolated and skeletal.

Of course I shouldn't have been anywhere near here. They'd been all too easily seduced, I think, by a whimsical mess-man and a mercurial cook, but the boys had loved the idea of a dinner. So I should by rights have been trawling the aisles of Asda. Or, at the very least, in Moseley, picking up a tie for tomorrow's court appearance. The two priorities with which I'd left the station, an hour ago. But instead I'd found myself down the better end of a fading Victorian suburb, trying to touch up past enthusiasms because the current ones had spooked me, that they are what they are. So there I was, pulled up in my little red Fire Brigade van, for all the world looking like a lost and confused Postman Pat. Sitting there as marinating time ticked by.

Back then, he was no more than a body to me, just my first fatal – something to be encountered and then moved on from, an inevitable and probably even necessary part of my nascent career. They'd found him eventually, after the fire had been put out and with nothing but the faintest wisps of smoke lingering in the dead spaces. He was in the toilet, an arm draped around the pan and his head laid back against the cistern. I'd been called up to take it all in, as though invited to a Danse Macabre; stood in the doorway, I tried to spool back to his final moments, whether on auto he'd crawled in here to try and puke, to sick away down the pan all the hot soot and carbon and shit that would have been pouring into his throat like a twisted inversion of a scream. He was a clammy, waxy grey but otherwise untouched, a silent, still rebuke to the inadequacies of my search technique.

They took the piss, of course they took the piss out of him: out of the Annie posters that were plastered all over the bedroom walls; out of the all too carefully bagged and boxed Smirnoff empties, dozens and dozens of them, like a cheap rent Howard Hughes; even out of him as he lay there, because of where he lay, because he'd ended up in the one windowless room of that sprawling house and so couldn't have leaned out, even if he'd have wanted to, to gasp at passing air. And I stood there, cluttering up the doorway, awkward and slightly numbed by it all. But I was slowly learning the ropes, the default defensive reaction to any stiff.

I suppose there was a good argument for it anyway, for me not having given much thought to him as an entity, nor to the violence of his final seven or eight minutes, or I might never have gone into a fire again, or never have cut another body out of a car. The clinical detachment, what may be construed as the callousness of poking a dead man with stick over his slightly suspect taste in musicals, didn't in any way seem to attenuate the professionalism and enthusiasm that any of us had for the job. Back then it seemed a necessary retort to death's sudden intrusion into my evening, to this impromptu evidence of its constant proximity; and pushing back against it with quips of increasing poor taste would become my default mechanism. Our default, as we attempted to out-quip each other. And yet here I am, now, pondering because of a jerk mix the foreshortened and empty and sad little life of a bloke who I probably never could have saved anyway, who was probably dead even before we'd turned out the station – imagining his history, the back story that had brought us together. Feeling an empathy that I haven't felt for a while, for anything, and now that it's back I'm finding it is somehow leavened with a regret as much for the realization of the lack in me as it is for him.

Perhaps it's all about resignation, in the end. Resignation to the dull attrition of the everyday, that we haven't learned to do. Perhaps systemic mismanagement is an inevitable and therefore to be expected element of all sprawling, hierarchical institutions. And that testing and polishing, when done conscientiously, open up a deeper and more profound satisfaction than I was ever able to access. Maybe it was the familiarity of her body that made sex so workaday, and not the third party intrusions that finished Louise and me. Maybe the practised indolence of which she thought us guilty should not have poisoned Rita and then her omelettes. The dull attrition that obscures the living of life.

Given the strange tenacity of this jerk project, I'm no longer sure of where I currently stand on the attrition scale, whether I'm guilty of making a net contribution to it or not. I do know that I can't face Asda's aisles this morning, the soullessness of it all, the bright sterility and impersonality of the process – the pea-green-and-black friendliness of the staff notwithstanding. Or is that really just another resignation failure on my part? Either way it's suddenly comfortable, this parody of Post-modern Pat, as the certainties with which I've been living, the surety of indifference, start to shudder and give way.

Why the toilet? Was he in there anyway, smashed on Smirnoff and therefore blissfully ignorant of it all, as it kicked off two floors below? It'd be a somewhat belated reassurance to think that he didn't finish with screaming lungs and bulbous, terrified eyeballs, but rather a slow, heavy-lidded drifting segue into oblivion, wanking, maybe, over Annie.

Little spots of rain pockmarked the windscreen. Over to the left, a couple of dog walkers had made their way across to the bandstand for cover, the threat of the coming shower a means to talk small and get to know. They were stood, by the disdainful look of them, in civic defiance of last night's condoms and butts and sharps – which is I suppose no stranger than anything else that any of us find to bond over. But time ticks on, and the Good Cop premium was beginning to bite. I'd still got a dinner to cater for.

On the corner of Cannon Hill Road, about a hundred yards up from where I was parked, there's a little open-all-hours that we've used before, late nights when the supermarkets have been closed. His stock's not bad, given the proportions of the place. I've always tried to steer clear of the back street places, if nothing else because of the ease of the one-stop Asda shop. Jumping around from place to place, negotiating traffic and parking restrictions, and then the sheer bloody annoyance of none of them having the stuff you want – it's all been grist to my apathetic mill. In the past. But whatever its drawbacks, it was beckoning to me that morning, loudly proclaiming its not-Asdaness with an outrageous spillage of fresh goods that tumbled out of the shop and onto the pavement, a great slop of green and purple and red pinching right up to the curb. It was like a Fifties' pastiche of an obsequious colonial handshake, an over the top eagerness trying to coax me in: a caricature, almost, a comic sketch of overspill. Or a goad to officious council clip-boards.

Fuck the rain, I thought. I'm not even gonna drive it. Bertie, you would be proud. In no time the little red van's door was locked and I was on my way up there, not entirely familiar with the purposeful intent of the walk that had suddenly taken me over, but getting into a stride anyway. You catch them a good twenty or thirty yards early, the threads of lemon and coriander and ginger spinning on the wind, as they throw up an alternative sensory bubble that neuters and then displaces all the shit of the city. The exoticism of the odour, the dissonance of primary colour reaches out to you, the chillies, aubergines, yams, all of them just piled up as they stand, poured into either drab brown boxes or cheap plastic trays. It's so Heath Robinson, so just thrown together, and yet it succeeds as an enormous inner city nosegay. I'd got years and years of accreted lassitude being smashed by a gaudy synesthetic truck. And all over the place, like litter on one of those summertime Calthorpe Park flower-beds, little tears of cardboard with pounds and pence graffitied in biro.

I'd been here before, of course, I'd passed in front of all of this to grab a bulb of garlic, a bunch of mint, but I'd never really seen it. The chaos, the energy, the facilitation of lives. He's got so much going on here that you have to zigzag a route via the benches and boxes to get through, and as I eventually reached out for the door, my elbow caught a tray of scotch bonnets that were balanced on a scaffolding-board bench. They must have been eight or ten fruits deep, and I couldn't resist plunging my fingers into them, feeling them close together at first and then give as I worked a way in. The whole of my hand swallowed by a potent, multi-coloured lucky dip. The plasticky pods felt synthetic as I continued to swirl through them, felt inedible, even as my other hand opened the door into the shop's gloom. It made me smile, thinking of left hands and right hands, as I caught sight of my Fire Brigade badge reflected in the glass. I took a bonnet and squeezed it until it began to weep a little, and then sniffed the brilliant smear that it had left on my fingers.

It was lit, the whole place, by nothing more than two strip tubes pushing back against a hoarder's gloom. Having just been seared by the colour outside, my retinas were taking a moment to adjust to the darkness that high, tight shelving imposes, but my nostrils had anyway taken over. Five spice and garam masala mixing with the chilli; perhaps it was a conscious effort of his, an appeal to the more primitive sense. Is it more primitive? Does it make it more likely that you'll spend in here? I brought my finger down from sniffing to licking, the sting of capsaicin rushing against my palate and up into my sinuses, and squeezed my eyes shut again. And then the tip of my tongue out again, in search of that fiery finger.

'Yes, my friend?' So with rheumy eyes I had to hunt around for him, trying to embody a voice, and eventually a withered old man came into view, stood behind a counter, looking up from an exotic script that he cannot possibly have been able to read in here. Again, and I couldn't help myself, but he reminded me of something out of Kipling.

'I'm after a jar of jerk mix? Or a packet? ... For marinating a chicken.'

'No, no my friend, we don't stock it. No point. It's all made up from scratch round here, from fresh stuff; they know that proper jerk comes out of a pestle, not a packet.'

'Bollocks. *Booolllocks!*' Ostensibly to myself, of course, and not an affront to his Earth Mother paean. To my unresignation. In a pitted and rusty convex security mirror that I could not for the life of me understand the need for, I saw the Good Cop premium, the suddenly onerous weight of being bothered. The withering of my rebirth. The anticipation of Rita. Do I bite the bullet and get up to Asda, despite myself? Or just dig out a curry sauce and be done with it? They're bound to do them in here, hidden somewhere in this half-light.

'No, no, it's worth it, stick with me here. Twenty minutes with a pestle and you'll never open a jar again. I'll show you how to knock it up.' And he shuffled out from behind his counter, a clutch of brown paper bags in an arthritic hand. 'I'll get you what you need. Come on, I'll show you. Couple of onions. Chop them; tiny dice is what you're after. Unless you have a ...' His voice faded as he made his way into the light. From where, exactly, was this enthusiasm coming? How was he picking up anything from the suddenly apathetic-once-more me, that was either sociable or solicitous? I followed him out anyway, and watched out of my disinterest as he moved between trays, filling his bags and murmuring instructions. 'Now, this isn't at all what normally goes into a West Indian jerk; you won't find it in any of the books, but they tell me it sings.' I wonder how long he's been here, cajoling his customers like this. Which is maybe just to distract myself from where he's taking me: I know she's going to be so pissed. I promised her a jar, promised her she had nothing to do, and I'm going to be walking out of this shop looking like the Green Man.

So I was stood outside a grocer's on a squally November morning as a little old man filled paper bags that I didn't want, explaining to me a recipe that I didn't see any point in remembering because there wouldn't be any point in passing it on. That my sulky hands stayed firmly pocketed seemed an impotent gesture. I looked down again to the van and the house. It's inconceivable that he wouldn't have shopped here, wouldn't have popped in on the way past for his fags and a loaf and a paper, on route to those lonely evenings in a one room bedsit. I wonder if he, too, came up against this cheeriness; whether that perky, rather irresistible force was around back then to wheedle himself into what the guy's life had become. Did they joke together and chew the fat as he asked for a packet of Benson and his litre of Smirnoff? Or did he just suffer it sullenly, parrying all that goodwill with a succession of grunts and defensive body language, insisting instead on looking at the tits on the front of *The Sport*? Did this little old Indian push his buttons or give him welcome cause to loiter? Seventeen, eighteen, must be close to twenty years but no more than a brief walk between me and this stiff who was still trying his hand at resuscitation.

Jesus, the air tasted good as I stood there, as though my taste buds, if nothing else, had been born again. But already I knew how this brief flirtation with interest would be ending. The pouty sulk that would threaten as soon as she saw me walking in there with my mass of sprouting paper bags, my fusion of bright smells, and then the mouth will thin away to nothing, tight and white. She'll not actually say anything, not to me; she'll have a selection of pans articulate her annoyance, slapping and smacking them around the kitchen in a perverse parody of intemperate Mediterranean creativity. And I guarantee she won't be grinding anything out into a paste; there'll be no recourse to any pestle, because I'm pretty sure that there isn't one on station.

So, in just a couple of hours, when I've finally gotten through the twitching death-throes of this enthusiasm aberration, we'll be back to our sullen status quo. And I shouldn't really have a problem with it, with being a mess-man manqué: it's a role known to have a short life expectancy anyway. I have the quiet time that will follow my resigning it to look forward to. But I just know he'll be there, Hidy, at the end, which is what's really pissing me off, on hand to finish that which he'd started at the beginning of the shift with his oh so innocuous suggestion of a jerk dinner. As she plates it: 'So it threatens to come good' – always so casual at first, so non-threatening – 'Just a little rapport with the kitchen crew is all it takes.' But that'll merely be the feint, him cranking it up for what he will already have found out to have been the catering failure, him setting the mise en scene for the actual non-consummation of another dinner. 'Mmmm . . .' as he joins the rest of them in pushing away a barely touched, barely recognisable Creole, and reaches across for the bread, '. . . and it could have come so rosy. Two quid that I had hoped not to give straight to the bin men.' And so he completes his work. I can feel it now, even before I've left this little corner shop, I can feel his cock inside me as the poisonous prick starts to shaft me, like he has some sort of droit de seigneur. 'I suppose the question remains; Where in any of this – other than the obvious, of course – where is there anything resembling anything jerk?'

I suppose I'm pissed that I'd allowed myself to be played by him, Hide the Snidy Bastard. The moment he sidled up and offered something that seemed constructive, I should have twigged. We are ever his playthings – Rita no more or less than anyone else – pawns in his malevolent matrix. His guile is effortless and bewitching to behold, a beautiful duplicitous conviviality that is no more than a means to bring our lips to the fruit. Maybe every watch has to have their Nigel. But then, maybe Eve should be asking herself why she'd felt the need to play.

7

I'm out of the habit of wearing ties. Or, until yesterday, even owning them. Since ending my full-on tryst with religion, only its vestigial rituals – weddings and funerals – and the odd bollocking at work get me four-square in front of a mirror, and even bollockings don't come along often enough anymore to keep me up to speed on all the variations on how to knot them. But then again, I had to wear a tie four times a week for more than twenty years and still knew only one of the apparently dozen or so ways of dressing a collar. Even though Mother said they should be, for me ties just weren't that important; a perfunctory twice round the standing part, through, in, and down, pulled hard enough to ensure that the tail corrugates like, I'm thinking now as I do it, like a tongue pursed against a swelling. Maybe if I'd thought of it like that then, as a swollen bud nestled between the pulled-back labia of a shirt's collars, maybe it would have interested me more, would have provided an amusing counterpoint to the 'Older Men', in their collars and the fashionable-at-the-time pink ties, as they declaimed the Lord's abhorrence of oral. Or maybe not. Maybe I was too angry.

But there can be no dwelling on the newly discovered clitoris this morning. Tying a tie for the first time in probably two years, I'm sat in front of my reflection in the window of the earlyish morning 61, and I realise that I can't do it anymore, I can no longer push through 'til three and four every night on the back of industrial quantities of Tennants, and then blag the day. The crows' feet I'm used to, the blotting webs of fine blood vessels in the cheeks surfacing like breaching whales. But today there's a sag I don't usually get to see, a lack of snap to the skin as it pools around and under my eyes in great marsupial pouches from which the eyes peek out, two foetal-red joeys. There's no pounding; my head hasn't pounded for years, just silts up in a gently shifting wooziness, a density, as everything desperately tries to induce some sort of dark, horizontal relief. Through the suspension, I sort of remember coming round as Cohen played on repeat into the headphones – 'Hey, that's no way / to say goodbye' – and quietly padding up the stairs and stripping off before going in, and gently inserting myself into her, carefully trying not to wake her, not straight away, as I thought of Lou.

It all feels pyrrhic now, all the little victories of logic and truth that the conflict and then the escape conferred. I'm still playing with my clit in the shitty window of the 61 as it crawls along the Bristol Road, heading towards the Law Courts and my ex, and what will probably be our last performance together in a cumless climax. At Bristol Street, everything still clogs up, surging and slowing, surging as they all push into the space that widens out in front of the lights. Suddenly I'm dreading that green-light release, that ejaculate, and yet for years I sat here willing it, desperate for it to throw me right on a pulse up the Middleway, with a flick of the rush-hour wrist. And now I am lately become a cock-ring of Children-in-Need sanctimony, dodging in and out of the slowing cars, holding everything back, insensible to the tumescence behind. He didn't seem to mind. He didn't mind the delay and the frustration, only the blankness of my greeting. I didn't recognize him, which he took for forgetting, but I never forgot Carlos. Carlos introduced me to sex, though he never knew and couldn't have known it, because I had to hide it from us. For years I had him lying on the hard tarmac of the playground, plucked from games in his house-colour tee-shirt and white shorts, his always thirteen-year-old hands tied behind him, his always thirteen-year-old eyes looking over, plaintively. Seeing him last week brought it all back. I was the marker. My task was to mark, to inscribe a numerical code along the inside of his thighs as he lay there. Why he was lying there, why he had to be catalogued, my little fantasy didn't explore. It wasn't relevant; we never passed beyond the clinical discharge of that inscriptive duty.

Perhaps understandably, the Semitic connotations of numbers on limbs passed me by; the whole penis dynamic was, for me, one of circumspection, not circumcision. How could it have been otherwise: even though there was at the time an enormous phallus rising up out of the front of the Watchtower magazine, and therefore a phallus in our hands as we went door-to-door and a(nother) phallus in our laps as we studied the lesson every Sunday, a veritable adoration of the peni, JWs don't do cock on cock – they don't do cunnilingus, for God's sake – so it was always going to be subject to some sort of denial. Inscribing got me on to his legs, got me actually touching the silky smoothness of those adolescent adductors, oh holy of holies, but without so much as a pass at a Rubicon. The five little depressions that the tips of my fingers made as they pressed into his skin were just the necessary steadying counterpoint to the movement of the marker, no more than a restraining adjunct to the ties behind, and nothing to do with wanting to fuck him. Desire satisfied through the exercise of power, replayed and revisited because – detached from the erotic – it was somehow, perversely, sanctioned contact. You forged the synaptic connexion between sex and control, and it's become a theme, Carlos, thank you.

Fantasising about tying up and writing all over Carlos couldn't sustain a patina of chastity forever, of course, and he soon led me into teenage thoughts – and then the accompanying teenage deeds – that were overtly sinful. I eventually did away with the cover of pens. For the most part it was secret sinning, except maybe when during an especially un-Witness reverie I split my foreskin and delivered a small but angry cock's worth of blood all over the sheets. But it was always a very Catholic pleasure, bound up with disappointment and self-loathing; each pulse of cum seemed to draw out with it a simmering guilt, like a poultice, or someone sucking out snake-bite venom. For the years it took me to build up an explanation for an escape, it seemed that Jehovah was collecting each semen-sodden sock as though it were a notch on His bedpost, in some sort of divine parody of my own power-play dynamic.

The dynamic withers before the Law Courts. It's good to get off, I hate buses, but stood in front of the imposing Victorian confidence of Webb and Bell's Welsh terracotta, and the arbitrary, ineluctable power of the magistrate within it, I feel more vulnerable than did any of my bound paramours, real or wished for. I adjust the clitoris once more, a little squeeze and a pull, and walk up.

*

'How great is the honour, Jehovah, to build you a place for your name! / We offer it now with rejoicing to add to your glory and fame.' We'd sing it with a shrillness that matched its banality: 'May we present this place to you, and here may your name be known. / We dedicate this place to you; please accept it as your own.' I haven't heard that for a dozen years at least, yet the moment I'm back here, I have those notes plinking in my head. They had it as part of the soundtrack at John and Sally's wedding, mood music spilling out through the open double doors. John Snr was humming along, his lips framing the unvoiced words like an incantation, as though it was somehow sacrilegious to let the tune go forth naked without its vocal accompaniment. Okay, it was his son's wedding; maybe you can explain it by the emotion of the day. 'And now may we honour you, father, by filling this place with your praise. / May glory ascend with the increase of those learning your ways.' I remember watching from the embankment, under the spread of sycamore, where every spring a rash of daffodils would nod in time to our supplications, our deference, our enforced acceptance of all those false prophecies.

It's the songs that stick, that have their barbs most deeply embedded, and they still generate a warm association that is totally at odds with the emptiness, and the error, of the sentiment in them. When I was about seven, they went through a brief phase – foreshortened maybe because they didn't realise how powerful it was – of having us kids sing the verses alone, with the adults joining in for the chorus. Our wavering castrato was immediately taken up and made strong with a surging tide of adult noise, an overwhelming demonstration of power and reassurance. I felt beholden, safe and belonged. My individual frailty had been both exposed and redeemed by an invincible, adult rescue refrain. I remember actually being tearful, a seven-year-old proto-addict. I, at least, had the oblate excuse. But the adults, the converts, providing all that protection?

Perhaps there's little time for a slow, nuanced accretion of personal belief when the End is so nigh. An urgent eschatology needs a blunt clarity; hence the constant beat of stripped back dogma, untroubled by aesthetics or pleasure, the ABC hymning that bookended each of the meetings. But maybe it's just the format; maybe if they composed them in Latin, or chant, even these hymns could accrue some gravitas. If you were to read fundamentalist transcriptions of Bach, maybe they'd sound vacuous. Maybe I've just got a downer on JWs.

I first jumped the fence after the split with Louise – I felt they owed me, or something, given their involvement in our marriage. Initially, it was just to subvert, to do something to fuck them over, to transgress, however timidly. Just strolling the grounds out of hours was enough when for twenty years you've been brought up always to defer to Mother. But it has become more than that: those bastard songs succour me, the easy familiarity of a world they conjured – ordered and controlled and purposeful – is soothing and placating. All that overarching, eventual justice. I pity them, I hate the proscriptivism, but whenever stuff stands close I still find myself wandering these grounds and remembering the nursery rhymes that we sang here and the associations they enable. A poisonous wet nurse, I know, but a tit's a tit. Though I don't think throwing in my hand as mess-man really qualifies. I was just passing.

It's a two-bit, asbestos ex-army mess hut, regulation grey, appropriated in the 50s and turned over to the Lord's work; no better example of sword into plough-share. And as ploughs go, it's pretty perfunctory; I suspect the actual austerity of the building would have struck some sort of chord when they'd first seen it, the Older Men charged with buying it. It would have chimed with the lean, pared-back, anti-High Church ethic of the Organisation. A pretty standard Protestant ethic, I suppose, though such a generic association wouldn't have been especially welcome to them. But, despite our would-be asceticism, I remember us struggling when winter laid bare its rudimentary heating, and we had to find a way of transubstantiating discomfort, by way of faith, into endurance: 'Please judge me, lord, observe my loyalty; / Observe my trust in you and my integrity', as we hoped that that trust would soon translate into spring. Squaddies, it would seem, are evidently a hardier collective than Witnesses. But still we held out in there against the cold and the indifference of the Devil's society, and it became our own miniature New World Order. After Sunday's Watchtower, a cabal of the faithful would busy themselves in the little kitchenette at the back, prior to sallying forth into the territory to preach. A dozen battered mugs, Tupperware sugar- and coffee-pots, and powdered milk, unction against the imminent animosity of the unsaved. We kids were indulged with hot milk and chocolate-chip biscuits. Or, in the autumn, we'd be deployed to strip the solitary damson tree before the locals did, to share out an earthly, rather than the longed-for spiritual, harvest to the faithful. We tidied the gardens, cut the grass, involved ourselves in all the mundane affairs of the Hall like Little House on the Prairies. Opportunities, when we hit pubescence, to mix with the hitting-pubescence Sisters. It was an alternative community, an alternative reality, obviating the need to touch the worldly one that was soon to be destroyed at Armageddon, all of it to be conscientiously avoided because 'I do not sit with wicked men of lies. / I hate the company of those who truth despise.'

But I haven't a tune accompanying the end. It was here, in an ante-room that I can now see was a parody of my isolation from the Organizational mainstream, that it finished, and it's wholly without a musical score. Confronting twenty years of implanted subservience, of deference to the Elders and the Matriarchs that policed the aisles, I reckon a staccato, shrill, dissonant psycho score would suit nicely, but all I have to pull it back into view is a view through a window. There's the place where I stood desperately willing myself not to defer any longer, not to yield to their supplications and assertions, not to believe that I was guilty of the 'spirit of independent thinking' that was Aaron's downfall when he was caught murmuring against Moses, just because I could no longer accept that Adam and Eve were an animation of Jehovah's breath and not the product of an adapting, value-free process of purposeless mutation. It was a stuttering stand, deferential in spite of my certainty and even the anger, but at the end of it I'd managed to burn every bridge coming out of that little room.

8

There's a scene in *Unforgiven*. A whore is pinned down and has a blade run repeatedly over her face, so that in place of a money shot you get threads of congealing blood. Shadowed as it is by impotence, someone once said, the burden of masculine potency exacts a heavy price.

'Well, she did laugh at his cock.' Phil attempts a leavening humour.

'So she didn't have it coming, then? ' Gemma, walking through after an evidently lazy session in the gym, is still in her shorts, her long legs stoppered by socks that are concertina'd down the way I like to think she knows I like them. Into the kitchen and then back to join us for supper, quotidian acts of ambulance. Perched on the edge of the seat, she pulls her knees together like a purse string, to balance the tray. There it is, that delightful scoop of biceps femoris dropping down away from the back of the knee, flaccid and smooth at rest. Davey P acknowledges her by turning over and snoring, just once, deliberately, provocatively, unable it seems to forgive her that pantomime caricature. Yet she's never been a confection of everyday beauty but a bitty, pitted thing of thought, a context, the history of that which I project on to her. She is a flickering screen playing my experiences.

'I'd still fuck her, though. Even cut up. Especially cut up, 'cos she'd be that grateful she'd want it.'

Lithe and gracile, I bet they'd part easily, be quick to wrap around, quick to open wide. Her knees would bend and pull up reflexively, each one into itself, and then she'd push them down into the giving mattress to offer up her cunt, and the effort raises her adductors into little ridges that accentuate the hollows of the pelvis either side of the pubic bone. I trace them down to where they disappear into the thigh, stroke them, stroke the inflexion where the long weight of the femoris hides itself away. Her skin is a delicate patterning, a kaleidoscope of subtle hues, the veal-calf white that runs down the inside of the thigh segueing into the blues and pinks around and under her knees. She's insensible to them, these simple things of propulsion and mobility, to their sexual capital.

'Why's that, Phil?' Dave surfaces from his faux slumber. 'Why'd she be grateful? Being slashed doesn't suddenly make you queer.'

'Eh?'

'You're a cunt, Phil. Unless she's suddenly turned to licking lettuce, why'd she actually want to be fucked by the biggest twat in the room?'

It is in fucking that we meet ourselves: it's where we come up against our deepest emotions. Anger, insecurity, tenderness, regret; all of life is focused upon and distilled into that first pulse of come. Every thrust pushes us a little further on to The Couch. And now, after the violence of the fucking, as I'm seeping into her like the blood that slowly spreads out from a wound, still she would be opening up, opening wider, as wide as the ties would allow, stretched and open and exposed, inviting and collaborating with the act, the subjugation. The aftershocks rippling through her body. She eroticises the visceral, animalistic exploration of power and surrender implicit in the deed, and that momentary capitulation to the past. What does it mean to want this?

9

It always was beautiful in winter, the patch of land that swamps the little 50s mess-hut. It banks and falls away, folds and puckers in an echo of the earth-moving of sixty years ago, so much bigger than it needs to be. The early winter frosts have given it an ethereal, never-never-land charm.

They tend it – we always tended it – religiously, as an offering to the Lord. Keeping the gardens as much as spreading the word was sanctified work, all of it a way to praise God. And it does have an impact, the moment you turn into the place – the crew-cut grass, the borders, the pots, all drawing the eye up to the sign above the doors, the first of many welcomes that any newcomer can expect: 'Kingdom Hall of Jehovah's Witnesses'. From over here, from beneath the sycamore, you appreciate the great, wide sweep of the path up to it, the girth of three wheelchairs, maybe. Which is ironic, really; it was they who taught me that 'strait is the gate, and narrow is the way, which leadeth to life'. Thought someone might have noticed that when they were laying it.

I wasn't the only one to have seen it as a Broad Road out. Clare Berry paraded herself up and down here, before and after every meeting, intent on limiting as much as possible the time that she was required to spend in there. And then she bailed, as soon as she was 16, after which we started referring to her as 'Clare Buried'. Sat on the bank amidst the disapproving daffodils with Tristan, I remember watching her modelling the white socks and short (as she dare) skirts that were de rigueur 80s, back and forth along the way that leadeth to destruction. She was striking, very, very pretty, and of course we fancied her anyway because she was older, and because she had what we thought to be so much ballsy independence. But we had to be discreet in our affections; she was known to be 'worldly', and we were vessels sanctified to the Lord, full-time ministers-in-waiting.

Even though her name suggested a ripeness, she was more like the untouched flower than the fruit. All that carefully projected knowingness and bravado was inevitably undone by her congenital condition: JWs on the run don't make good ingénues, though it's generally not for want of trying. She came on to me once, a teasing fumble rather than with any intent, bold in the knowledge that it could not and would not go anywhere. Her nails dragged through my hair, down my face, my chest – leaving little red furrows wherever they caught the exposed skin. She followed them south until she was kneeling before me, a frustrated fourteen-year-old's clumsy parody of what she thought a 'bad girl' was. Her hands rested tentatively on my hips, and she took in her teeth the cotton of my fly, gave it a gentle tug before looking up coquettishly, her eyes wide as planets, and then gave me a crooked smile. I could think only of Betty Boop. She did it for the transgressive frisson: this was one of the periods in which fellatio was banned, and not just for fourteen-year-olds. Forgive her, for she knows not what she does; she probably didn't even appreciate the significance of that which she was parodying.

But maybe, even back then, maybe she did; maybe she – maybe they – had intuited the relationship between the broad, destructive road and sex. Maybe fucking is nature's riposte to the Godhead, its counter-claim over the inexorable, evolutionary perfecting of man. Its conclusive, concussive counter-punch. Maybe fellatio is the first capitulatory step to the bestial, and the id has soft lips. Maybe she knew, even as she knelt before me in pseudo-supplication, that I too would soon be bending the knee before the great god Cum. And that maybe God, Jehovah, through His Witnesses alone, stands point.

The daffodils aren't standing point at this time of year. Because they haven't dead-headed and tied them, they remain as withered vestiges of yellow and brown on the bank. Sat amongst them again, now, it's not so much Betty's eyelashes that I'm thinking about, nor the fingernails pricking through the pockets of my trousers, nor even those probably soft, probably idic lips, but her ankles as she knelt, two flashes of white signalling into the future. They framed her head, a pair of over-large hair bunches. Maybe I remember them so vividly because Lou so suddenly stopped emulating them.

And yet the Lord hates a divorcing.

I imagine her, the British racing green of her short-as-she-dare skirt and those almost compulsively adjusted white socks. Knelt before me, head bobbing, maybe not knowing what she does, for which I forgive her, as I cum beneath the sycamore, and I can feel the daffodils nodding.